Dreamers
in a Haunted House

Some people believe that a Ouija board gives them a contact with the dead. It was with this hope in mind that four people sat in seance one moonlit night in a deserted mansion. Gorse Manor was said to be haunted.

But its eerie reputation was not the reason for the visit. Harold Lunn's beautiful young wife had been found murdered there some time before, and he and a medium, plus a young man who had known the dead woman intimately, join Inspector Cartland in this last-ditch attempt to solve the murder—through the words of the murdered.

With four fingers placed on the cup, it begins to spin around the board and peck at letters. Strange things are said.

Books by Marc Lovell

DREAMERS IN A HAUNTED HOUSE
VAMPIRE IN THE SHADOWS
A PRESENCE IN THE HOUSE
THE IMITATION THIEVES
THE GHOST OE MEGAN

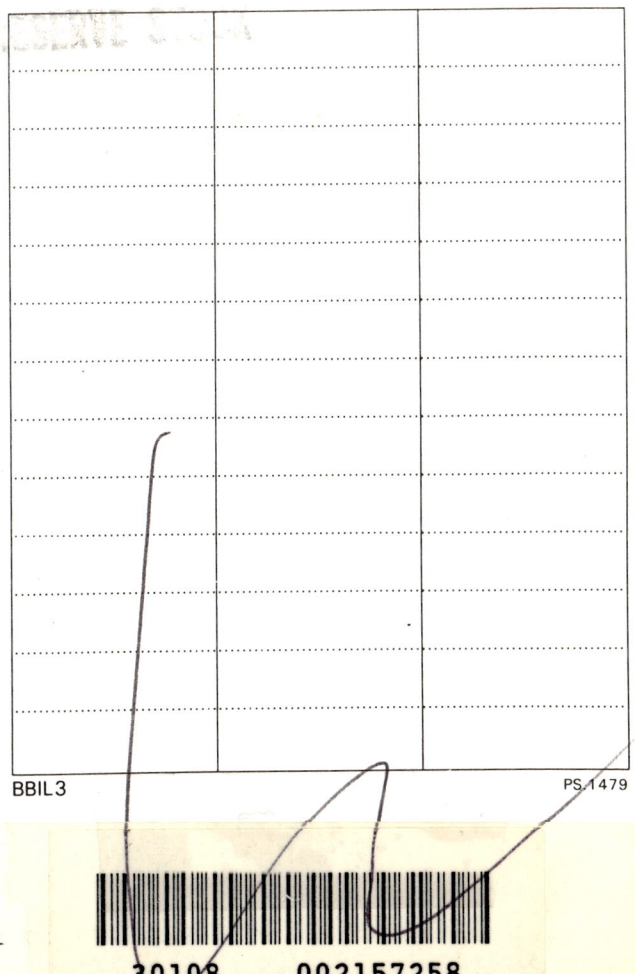

Dreamers
in a Haunted House

MARC LOVELL

LONDON
ROBERT HALE & COMPANY

Printed and bound in Great Britain by
REDWOOD BURN LIMITED
Trowbridge and Esher

Dreamers
in a Haunted House

Michael was afraid.

He had many reasons for being so. Too many reasons, in fact. Not for the first time since leaving the house, he was tempted to turn back. And this was only the beginning. There were greater fears to come.

A half moon lit the scene with a sinister paleness. It was like the light from a thousand hidden candles.

Michael was reminded of the way his childhood bedroom had been illuminated from the street-lamps outside, in the days before he got a night-light. Then he switched his mind away before remembering how, at eleven o'clock, the lamps went out and he was left in the dark. He had always been afraid of the dark.

Michael Shield was slowly pedalling a bicycle along a stretch of country road. On either side were dense thorn hedges. Trees leaned over, silent and unmoving in the still air. There was silence everywhere, apart from the faint moan of his bicycle.

Michael wished he were back in the suburbs of Stilton, back there five minutes ago, with houses and brightness and noise. He had felt fine then, adventurous. He could have stayed like that forever, pedalling toward but never reaching the imminent fears.

From behind came light, a violent splash. It was trailed by the growing sound of a car.

The tightness of Michael's breathing eased. He welcomed the wavering light, took comfort in the appearance and fast growth of his own shadow on the road before him. It was as if he were chasing a trembling monster.

His shadow leapt aside as the car passed. Michael noted that it was a new model, the 1937 Austin VII. He had always been interested in cars, liked knowing the different models and makes. Someday he was going to learn to drive.

Michael amended: No, that was before. The future is dead.

A thrill of anticipatory pleasure ran up his legs, shot through his bowels, seared his spine. The smile brought by the thrill was as loose and natural as a daydreaming infant's.

He didn't mind so much now that the car had taken its sound and light away. The glance he spared the yellow glow of his lamp was forgiving.

It was another minute before the fear came back.

The hedge on his right had ended. It had been replaced by a wall of crumbly brick. Some three feet high, it was topped by tall iron railings with spiked heads. Beyond were trees.

His legs turning the pedals even slower now, Michael rounded a bend. There ahead of him stood the gatehouse.

It was a low piece of Victorian Gothic, with heavy pediments and leaded windows and browbeating eaves. The building formed one side of the gateway, the other being a sturdy pillar on top of which squatted a griffin with a raging mouth. The gates, as always, were open.

One of the small, staid windows in the gatehouse showed light behind its curtain; dimly, a prim offering; it matched the architectural era. The glimmer seemed to suggest that although passion lay within, it should only be hinted at.

Staying on the road, Michael averted his eyes as he went by. Knowing the act to be foolish made no difference. It was reassuring, his notion that what was not seen couldn't see.

The railings continued past the gatehouse, around another bend, and went on out of sight when Michael came to a gentle, reluctant stop.

Dismounting, he switched off the lamp and lay his machine in the weeds which grew in the yard of space between roadside and wall. He brought out a handkerchief to wipe the dampness from his hands.

Michael Shield was twenty-six years old. He was tall but

had a slouch, a diffident droop of the upper body, a trait common in the overtall yet rare in those who owned merely two inches over the average height. It was a soft body, plump and paunchy. His weight was accentuated by the tight fit of his suit—double-breasted blue serge—a tightness more acute than the fashionable. The collar of his grey shirt looked equally undersized and the knot of his tie was no bigger than a thumbnail.

Michael had a round, smooth face. It could have passed for that of someone in the late teens. There was that tremulous look to the pouty lips and the bulbous cheeks, that young shapelessness of the nose, that uncertainty of beard and traces of pimple scars, that unformed appearance of the whole. The fingers of firm, decided character had not yet set to work on moulding the waiting putty.

He had dark fine hair as neatly parted and brushed as a boy's on his way to Sunday school. It matched Michael's eyes in colour and manner. They were attractive eyes, a saving grace. Not that the rest of the face was unappealing, simply not worthy of first attention.

Michael's eyes, deep brown, had a penetrating gaze which could be either disturbing or an allayer, depending on the recipient. He seemed to be looking through or into. A cast of bemused anxiety suggested that what he sought was the good, because he wanted proof of his belief that it was there. His eyes had innocence and kindness, worry and sadness.

Usually. Now they were dull with fear.

Michael put his handkerchief away and moved on from where he had left the bicycle. Ten steps brought him to a place in the rails where one of the uprights was missing. The space was eighteen inches across.

Gloves, he told himself.

He reached into his jacket pocket, touched the rumple of thin leather, felt satisfied with the gesture, and brought his hand out again.

It took him less than half a minute to squeeze through the

gap in the railings. He knew that because he checked his watch before and after. The time, he noted, was nine-fourteen.

He moved on from the rails.

The trees were larch and pine. Standing close, they tangled arms with each other like wrestlers caught in the beginning of the act.

It was darker here. The waxing moon managed to penetrate only with shafts of flashlight slenderness. Michael went slowly, his hands slightly raised at either side.

He found difficulty in believing what was happening. It was hard to accept that he, Michael Shield, was here by choice. Here walking in fear, heading for terror, knowing that at last would come horror.

But yes, it was true. And it had to be.

The going underfoot was easy. Rabbit runs made natural paths in the low flora. There was a rank smell of rotting undergrowth.

Michael heard a sound. It was like a soft handclap.

His reaction was swift. His arms shot up to clasp across the pain in his chest, his head went down, his knees sagged. He stayed taut and trembling in this elongated foetal position, mouth in a wide-stretched clamp, eyes closed. His heart pained and pounded.

Another sound came, trailed by a fading slither.

A rabbit, Michael insisted to himself. Only a rabbit. Or a dog. Or a cat. Sheep. Bird. Grass snake.

His panic eased. He straightened slowly. He ran damp hands hard down the sides of his jacket and then pressed against his hips, touching there the ache of indecision.

Drawing a deep, quivering breath, he forced himself to move forward.

His eyes now were more dartingly alert than before. He couldn't resist the fast searches in every direction, even though he dreaded a find. He would have preferred to gaze at the ground, or keep his eyes slitted.

A holdover from childhood, unkillable by adult logic, was Michael's belief that in the darkness inanimate objects came to life. He might scoff at the conceit by smiling day, but, circumstances being unfavourable, it returned creepingly at night.

A table became a strange creature on long legs, waiting for the right moment to pounce. Chairs crouched. Pictures watched him from where they gripped the walls. Rugs lay ready to roll and ensnare.

There was always movement. Often in the past Michael had turned suddenly on an object, his notice of it putting a stop just in time to the stealthy shifting which he had glimpsed from the corners of his eyes.

The night was evil, Michael knew.

The trees began to thin out. Ahead lay the brightness of unhindered moonlight. Michael hurried forward.

He came out of the trees. He was on open ground. It had once been a lawn, was now an expanse of lumpy weedland with, in the centre, a fallen statue.

Beyond, one hundred yards from the trees which circled the estate, stood the house.

Gorse Manor. It was of the same Gothic pattern as its gatehouse guard. There were two main floors, and a row of dormer windows above the ornate eaves. Each end sprouted a turret, a pointed, pornographic butte of mouldy brickwork. The entrance was up a crescent of steps which supported a pillared portico, itself also semi-circular.

Michael looked at the house as he moved toward it over the open ground. More than looked: stared. He had seen the place once before, in the daytime. It had appeared dead and sinister then. Now it had a corrupt vitality.

Yet he kept moving forward. He wondered if he were dreaming. It was possible, he thought. He held to the thought. It helped.

He came to the statue. Pausing, he looked down. The figure had broken off just below the knees. It lay on its back, sightless eyes open, nose eaten away by the elements, fingers gone from the upstretched hands. Representing a child, a girl of perhaps ten, the statue seemed to be making an appeal to heaven.

Michael, unknowingly shrinking back, reminded himself that in her proper position the girl would merely be holding her arms out, possibly in an offering gesture.

He turned away quickly. He thought he glimpsed . . . But no. No, there had been no movement. He went on.

Underfoot turned to a hardness. Gravel. He was on the driveway, which came from the gates and formed a turnabout here in front of the manor. Discernible as such by daylight, despite the spread of ground-hugging weeds, now it seemed a continuance of yesteryear's lawn.

The house loomed above him, menacing. The impression of threat grew the closer he went. He clenched his fists.

Proximity made the steps clear. There were five. They had been forced to unevenness, an ugly clash of levels, by the short tough grass which grew from the cracks.

Michael reached the steps and went up. The rubber soles of his shoes made no sound on the stone. There was no sound anywhere. Even so, the silence seemed to deepen as Michael passed under the portico and into its shadow.

In front of the door he stopped and took a deep, calming breath. He bent down to search among the tufts of grass fronting the doorstep. Pushing one tuft aside, he saw the glint of new metal.

The key.

Leaving it there, he straightened and brought out his gloves. He found difficulty in drawing on the first, which made him wonder if they were too small. Then he reminded himself they had been a perfect fit when he had bought them last week. It was the damp of his hands, he realised.

Working steadily, he gathered comfort from the needed concentration. He was sorry when the job was done.

Still in charge of his comfort, he stooped swiftly and got

the key, rose and fitted it into the lock. He twisted his hand. The key turned smoothly and quietly.

Now Michael hesitated, comfort gone. Now the terror was to begin. He didn't know if he could go on. What would he do if . . . ?

Gorse Manor was haunted. Everyone knew it. Michael knew it. There had been so many stories. It was not simply gossip. The last tenants, ten years before, had stayed only a week. Others had lasted less. The caretaker, the woman who lived alone in the gatehouse, would enter the place only on Sunday mornings, when she gave a fast airing and cleaning to parts of it at a time. There was no doubt in the matter. Gorse Manor was haunted.

Michael's belief in ghosts was total. He accepted that they were spirits of the dead. There was no titillation involved. He could not, as many could, read a ghost story for the chill pleasure it gave. He could not read such a story at all. And he had always avoided hearing details of the Gorse hauntings, or any other. He was terrified of his belief, which was the ultimate for him of all that had a traditional connexion with night.

He closed his mind to possibilities. He whispered, "I am dreaming. I am in my bed at Piper Street. I am asleep and dreaming."

His heart beating fast, Michael pushed open the door and stepped through. He was distantly proud of his bravery.

On the inner threshold, he found himself in a large baronial hall. Amply lit by moonlight shafting in from windows above and behind him, it was exactly as it had been described. He received a faint shock of recognition.

The hall was two stories high. Galleries ran along the upper level. They were reached by a staircase which rose at the far end and forked halfway, curving off to serve either side. Below were doors interspersed with high-backed chairs and pictures in heavy frames. There was nothing in the centre, only the vast spread of black and white tiles.

Dwelling on his bravery, Michael turned and got the key, put it in his pocket, and gently closed the door. It gave a light thud.

He turned again to face the hall and began to move forward, heading for the staircase.

Suddenly, the sensation of being trapped came about him. His fear bloomed to terror like a flower bursting from bud. He was attacked by so many facets of dread that he became dizzy, confused about which enemy to fight.

His breath wheezing its tightness, hands clasped on his chest, he kept moving slowly forward while watching from the periphery of his vision chairs and doorways making sly movements; while suffering the prickling of his back which made him want to whirl and protect himself from its cause, the silent and smiling follower; while jabbering in thought that he would never get out in time because his gloved hands would fumble with the catch and taking the gloves off would be too hard, too slow; while aware of being watched by a hundred secret eyes whose guiding minds were devising evils; while telling himself that all this was an elaborate trick (or a dream, a dream, a dream); and while waiting in dread confidence for the appearance of a ghost.

He saw one.

Michael stopped and gagged on a cry and felt a huge pain lurch through his chest.

The figure, dim, stood in a doorway to the right of the staircase. The figure was male, and undoubtedly there. Michael knew he was not imagining its presence. This was not like the way he felt about objects coming to life—that was another kind of conviction. The figure was there.

He could see it clearly, had seen it move into the doorframe. The light was too poor, the distance too great, for the picking out of details, features. The figure was merely a male form, standing quietly, watching.

And then it was gone. It slid back from view.

Michael's terror, unlessened by the retreat, offered him

three choices: collapse, a run for the door, an escape from the vicinity by going ahead.

He was kept from the first by the dreadful thought of lying unconscious and defenceless. The second was abnegated by a picture of himself fumbling with the door. It had to be the third.

Michael snapped forward. He wanted to run but couldn't. He was unable to get his limbs to move with swift smoothness. He marched jerkily, a toy.

It was that familiar nightmare ploy of body disobeying mind, and the inference of dreaming again came to Michael's aid.

It enabled him to pass the suspect doorway and resist the insane urge to look through; to go to the stairs and start up; to push the terror back down to fear; to stand the thought of his back being unprotected to what was below.

Where the staircase forked, Michael made to the right. He reached the gallery. Movements smoother now, closer to a semblance of normalcy, he went along past three closed doors. The last door in the row was open.

He stopped there and looked into a spacious study. It was lit by moonlight. There were tables, chairs, a couch, bookcases. In front of the large fireplace stood a leather wing-chair.

In that chair sat a woman. She was in profile. She had long white hair and wore a white garment. Her hands were clasped in her lap.

Michael went into the room. His attitude became stealthy. As he drew closer to the wing-chair his hands moved forward. His eyes were unblinking.

The woman made no movement.

Michael came to a stop behind the chair and rested his hands on its top. He released a heavy sigh.

Slowly, the woman got up. She turned.

"Yes," she said. "That's all right."

———— ◆ ————

As a girl, Rosalind lived in a pleasant street lined with trees. The houses were three-bedroom units with mock-Tudor façades. There were neat front gardens and sparkling windows and the curtains were always straight.

It was an unwritten law of the neighbourhood that all signs of indigence should be reserved for the rear, where junk and disarray and age-dim drapes detracted in no way from the mock-sturdy brickwork.

Rosalind was the family pet. Not only was she the youngest, not only was she the sole girl, she was also the only one who had inherited the darkness of an Irish grandmother.

She became proud of this mark of distinction. Later, it helped put the metaphorical edging of ermine on her cloak of dreams; a cloak of royal purple; she wore it constantly.

Rosalind's feeling was positive that she had a quality which set her apart from all others. No one in the whole world, she thought, could have understanding such as hers, so complex a body of emotions, a perception as profound.

That ninety-five out of every hundred intelligent young people had exactly the same feeling of being special, Rosalind never realised. Furthermore, her feeling was to continue. She went on wearing at least the lining of her cloak in adult life, the harshness and disillusions of which failed to rend holes in the mystic cloth.

Both her parents worked, mother in a bank, father as an elementary-school teacher. But there was never enough money. The necessities barely scraped through to being sufficient. Fires were small. Gifts were handicrafts. Vacations were spent hiking and tenting.

"We can't afford it, darling," was the answer Rosalind always received when she wanted a dress like Mary's, a new bicycle like Joan's, or to go to a private school like those girls in the next street.

The answer was infuriating. She would stamp her feet or break an ornament or retreat coldly into her specialness. It was a form of noblesse oblige which made her smile again, accept the consoling kisses and the promises of "someday."

At sixteen, Rosalind started going out with boys. She was popular, pretty, and had a pleasant manner. The gawky youths took her for walks and to the cinema and to sixpenny dances in church halls. Her parents were disapproving. They said she was only a child.

Rosalind enjoyed her dates. She would chatter of non-existent piano-lessons and holidays in Brighton. She would pretend the drab dance-hall was a glamorous supper club. She would give her date a romantic background and ignore his pimples. She would imagine her dress was not her mother's taken in but a new gown from London.

On her seventeenth birthday she met Harold Lunn. She was dazzled by his worldliness. Already at twenty-four he was a partner in his father's accountancy business. He lived in Stilton, a medium-sized town thirty miles away across the Warwickshire border.

He owned a car.

They met at a bring-and-buy sale, which Rosalind had easily turned into an Eastern bazaar. Her date, a gulping youth of blushes, was forgotten when Harold Lunn had been introduced and promptly bought her some home-made chocolates. Out of the hearing of flushed ears, Harold and Rosalind made a date for the following night.

When, a week later, she took her new boy friend home, Rosalind was embarrassed by the fuss her parents made of him. Abundantly, they approved. They plied him with tea and cakes and questions.

Afterwards, in a bewildering switch from their stand of a few months earlier, they told their daughter that she was almost a woman and should start thinking of the future.

She and Harold Lunn courted. Driving over every week-end, he took her to real dances in real ballrooms, to restaurants with waiters, to dress-circle seats at the pictures. He bought her presents. He flattered her by conversing with her on esoteric topics as though she were an equal in maturity.

It was all very satisfying, like sunshine, except that she felt she had nothing to give in return. There was, of course, sex, that intriguing fact of life which nobody talked about. Rosalind would have been ready to allow Harold the total freedom of her intimacy had he pressed the matter. He never did, therefore neither did she. If Harold was content with the circumspect gropings of couch and car seat, then so was Rosalind. She concluded that her company was return enough.

One evening while they were strolling in town, Harold said, "I bought a ring today."

"Oh?"

"It's an engagement ring."

"I see," she said, feeling funny inside.

"I'd like to give it to you, if you'll accept it."

"Yes, I will."

He drew her to a stop and looked down at her gravely. "I want you to marry me, Rosalind."

She nodded. "I will."

"I love you. Do you love me?"

She said, "Yes, Harold, I do."

Rosalind was lying. And she knew it. Although she was still dazzled, she did not love Harold and felt sure she never would. He couldn't see her cloak. Probably she would never meet anyone who could. However, she was fond of her fiancé, knew he would be hurt if she backed out, and there was no one else she liked more.

They got married.

After the church service, everyone went back to the bride's home for thin watercress sandwiches and tea. Rosalind was radiant when Harold drove her away.

Despite grey weather and the surprising disappointment of sex, the honeymoon in Portugal was a success as far as

Rosalind was concerned. The trip, in fact, was the greatest, most profound success of her life. The dazzling she received, compared to that from Harold, was as a searchlight to a candle.

Rosalind fell in love. The recipient was foreignness and the concept of travel. It was to remain her strongest passion, next to that for the secret person whom nobody knew but herself.

The house in Piper Street, Stilton, a wedding present from Mr. and Mrs. Lunn, Sr., was the same size as and almost identical design to Rosalind's old home. But it was new. It was a good beginning, Rosalind felt.

She was content those first few years of the marriage. She enjoyed cooking and doing her own housework, took pleasure in Harold's appreciation of these. She had ample free time. The annual fortnight abroad was marvellous. She was never short of pocket money. Sex became pleasant. It was a relief that Harold was as disinterested as she in having children. She had every comfort. She was able to dress well and take care of herself.

Rosalind was a small, neat person. Not quite five feet tall, she had dainty hands and feet, and an inordinately slender waist which seemed even smaller because of the way her hips swelled roundly and her breasts pouted. It was an alluring, striking body, beautifully proportioned, complemented by pretty legs that had a girlish smoothness.

Although the fashion was for short hair, Rosalind wore hers long. It went straight back from a widow's peak, behind her ears, and dropped to a weak outward curl where it touched her shoulder blades; it always looked as though she had just climbed up the steps of a swimming pool with her head back. She kept it lustrous with frequent shampooings and a nightly one hundred strokes of the brush. Her hair had always been her chief vanity.

With less interest but similar dedication, Rosalind looked after her other points of external interest. Surgeon's gloves protected the finish of her expressive hands; her fingernails she had tended professionally once a week. She used mud-packs, the finest of cosmetics, and tried every "miracle" lotion that appeared on the market.

All this was more usual in women ten and twenty years Rosalind's senior. She herself sometimes wondered why she spent so much time on tasks she did not particularly enjoy. The only answer was her amorphous feeling that she must hold herself in readiness, that she must be prepared. For what, she didn't know.

The corporeal theme of daintiness and prettiness was continued in her face. Her features were small, doll-like. The dark eyes could, perhaps, have been a little larger; but apart from that faint complaint, there was no fault to be found. The face was sweet and composed and had a distant haughtiness that was appealing rather than offensive.

Four years passed before Rosalind began to get restless.

The seed had been sown in Lisbon, was watered by other trips abroad and visits to London, broke through the soil of satisfaction with the first yawn. The restaurants and ballrooms which had been glamorous in courtship days were now provincial and staid. Her home was achingly bourgeois. Ownership of a car was commonplace. Never being short of money lost its power through familiarity.

Naturally, Rosalind had long since ceased to be dazzled by her husband. He was complacent, without high ambition. His hair thinned and he grew a moustache. Every day he seemed to be sinking deeper into the parochial rut. Rosalind was depressed when he gave up cigarettes and started smoking a pipe, which made him seem even more stolid. His only hobby was silly. He had to get glasses for reading, and that in Rosalind's view was another flaw. They went out less and less.

Like greying, Rosalind's restlessness increased as time passed. She watched the seasons change and saw no change in her life. She was choked with envy when her family emigrated to New Zealand. The two-week vacation every August took forever to come around, was over in a flash, and left her sullen and withdrawn. She was withdrawn generally. She did have that basic security of her cloak.

When Rosalind was twenty-four, her mother-in-law died. Mr. Lunn died some months later. Harold became sole owner of the firm, as well as inheriting property.

Recovered from sadness over the loss of her in-laws, of whom she had been fond, Rosalind grew excited about the new development. She expected that now she and Harold would have more freedom, would travel more and get up to London often. She also expected that they would move to a different, larger house.

Harold, however, seemed content to continue as before. He liked his home, he said. As for the rest:

"Times are too hard for gadding about."

"Hard?" Rosalind said.

"Dear, don't you know we're in the middle of a depression?"

The acquisition of what she considered wealth had, Rosalind believed, turned her husband into a miser. They went out even less than before. Harold spent countless evenings at home, slumped in a chair, reading ledgers, spectacles on, puffing at his pipe. It was a dreary picture.

Rosalind became nervous and irritable. Her housewifely duties suffered. She nagged and complained. She dyed her hair blond, which she disliked, but considered it to be the flag of her revolt. Squabbles grew frequent in the Piper Street house. They were always started by Rosalind.

She was not a bad woman. She was bored and foolish and spoiled. Mainly, she was crippled by the belief that a special destiny awaited her somewhere.

This it was that led her, eventually, to Gorse Manor one night in May of 1937.

———————◆———————

Rosalind rose slowly from the wing-chair. Turning, she said, "Yes. That's all right."

She looked at Michael closely. He was standing behind the

chair, his hands on its top. She noted the gloves. She also noted that Michael was tense.

He asked in a whisper, "You didn't hear?"

"Very little," Rosalind said. She kept her voice pitched at normal level.

"Good."

"You did well."

"Yes."

Michael was still whispering, which Rosalind didn't like. It irked her that he had not followed her lead. But she was unconcerned. She was glad the waiting had ended. She had been bored sitting here alone in the moon-dim room, and her feet were cold.

She drew closer across her throat the collar of her white raincoat, saying:

"What a big old gloomy house."

Michael nodded. He lifted his hands from the chair and clasped them together on his stomach. Slowly, only his head moving, he began to look around the room.

Rosalind wondered at his tension. It was still palpably present. She could think of no reason for it. Not yet. Later it would be understandable.

Through Rosalind ran a thrill of pleasure which made her shoulders twitch and her mouth abruptly smile. Blinking, she drew her lips back to composure.

Michael had not noticed. He was gazing about him as if with apprehension, like a dog that scents a cat.

Settling from her thrill, Rosalind thought how odd that appearances could be so deceptive. Here was Michael, the most mild-looking of men, and so different inside. So totally different.

But then, Harold gave a similar false impression. On the outside he was all the solid, unromantic, down-to-earth professional man. No one would guess, looking at Harold, that he had a fervent interest in the supernatural.

Harold Lunn was a tall spare person who owned a severity beyond his years. It was in his bearing, the way he carried himself and swung his arms; in the side tilt of his head when in the act of query; in his habit of pursing his lips on his bottom teeth—causing a dozen white hollows of pucker around his mouth; in the steeple-making of his long, bony fingers; in the close crop of his curly brown hair.

At home he wore Oxford bags and a blazer. For business, he was always in a dark suit, grey-blue tie, and rigid collar. Both outfits were ungainsayably conformist. There was no hint of the unorthodox about Harold Lunn.

He had a good-looking face. Long, it had a straight nose which rose grandly and smoothly from the high cheekbones like a kneed-up sheet. He had a firm chin. His eyes were warm and kind, a mildly startling contrast to the man's appearance and demeanour.

The life of Harold Lunn was made up of three elements. Outside these, little else touched him or roused more than a fleeting interest, be it the abdication of a king or a fire in the house across the street.

The first element was his profession. Metaphorically, he had cut his first tooth on a ledger. His earliest memories were divided between the nursery and his father's office on Stilton's High Street, a collection of small, dark, musty rooms where clerks with wing-collars moved quietly and spoke in undertones. There had never been any question in Harold's mind about his career.

The second element was his home. Which meant, of course, Rosalind. Harold loved his wife. He had fallen in love with her at first sight and had courted her strenuously, spending more than he could comfortably afford in order to impress her and have his love returned. He knew he had succeeded in the last when, after they became engaged, she responded so ardently to his lovemaking that it was obvious she was prepared to give in to him completely. He restrained himself. He was a highly moral man, as some educated non-religious people tend to be, cleaving to the locum princi-ples/commandments with all the convert's celebrated passion.

The third important element in Harold's life was the oc-cult. He had become intrigued with the subject during his last year at grammar school, when he and other boys, in search of sensationalism, a strident lack in their world, would get together of an evening for table-tilting—with as much success as if the tables were windmills. The craze passed (motorbikes took over) for all of them except Harold.

After going through Stilton public library's small collection of works on the occult and its relatives, he used his pocket money to send to London for whatever books were available, technical or fiction. He read everything avidly.

Hearing about the Society for Psychical Research, he made contact and became a member. It pleased him and increased his interest to learn that the organisation was so esteemed and venerable, having been formed on July 17, 1882, under the presidency of the noted Henry Sidgwick. There had been even older groups, Cambridge's Ghost Society and a Phas-matological Society at Oxford. He received the SPR's journal regularly and studied the case histories and investigations.

Harold was slightly left of centre, assuming the radical to be absolute belief in discarnate agency, which made him almost ideal as a researcher, or as merely an interested party.

He had never seen a ghost, or what may be termed such for the sake of convenience. He had never experienced psychical phenomena. His dreams, which he made note of diligently, always turned out to be what 99.9 of dreams are: wishful thinking. He failed at card-guessing, automatic writing, and other sidelines both gimmicky and useful.

He was not, Harold concluded, psychic in the smallest degree. Yet his interest thrived. In time, he grew astute enough to realise that his hobby supplied the mysticism which an atheist craved.

After his father's death, Harold's involvement with the occult became more pronounced. This was in order to form a welcome break from the many new problems with which he found himself beset in the other two elements of his life.

He had been willed three houses which were mortgaged and had unreliable, reticently paying tenants. The firm, which he also inherited, was in as feeble a condition as most other concerns in the grim mid-thirties; people either had no business to account, or were struggling with their own book-keeping to save the fees.

Harold was worse off than before, mainly because of the death duty he had to pay on both his parents. Regretfully, he put two of his clerks on half time, adding the rest of their work to his own. He cut financial corners with the abandon of a bad driver.

Aggravating matters was the behaviour of his wife. For some time now Rosalind had been restless and petulant. This Harold had blamed on her lack of interests outside the home. He tried, with no success, to get her to take up a hobby or become involved with community affairs. When, after his father's death, her irritability increased, he decided it was due to the fact that, suspecting his worries, she felt helpless and useless.

Harold had never discussed personal finance with his wife. Always he had given her the trite "Don't trouble your pretty head about it." Now it would be trouble indeed. *A problem shared is a problem halved* was an aphorism to which he didn't subscribe. He saw no reason to give worries to Rosalind while in no way reducing his own. Besides, he felt sure that the economy, having reached its nadir, was now on its way up.

It was about this time that Harold made the acquaintance of Mrs. Foster. She was referred to as a spiritualist but called herself a sensitive. She lay claim to no great supranormal powers.

"My gift is slight," she told Harold on their first meeting. He said, "I'm sure that's not true, ma'am."

"It is. But I keep trying."

Mrs. Foster's protestation was as refreshing to Harold as was her appearance. All other mediums he had come across had been loud in praise of their own metagnomy, while dressing like a cross between Mata Hari and an oriental princess. And they had all been fakes.

Mrs. Foster was a short, plump widow in her early sixties, a motherly person. She had a round red face and a cheery smile. Always she wore wrap-around aprons and headscarves tied in the fashion of a peasant. There were no bangles or beads; her only jewellery was a wedding ring. She looked as though she were about to go to market to sell eggs.

Her home was a cottage on the outskirts of town. There she held seances for which she made no charge. She was not a professional medium.

On further acquaintance, Harold soon realised that Mrs. Foster had underestimated her talent. She did indeed have a gift. He also discovered that she was a primitive. She had little knowledge of things parapsychological; she had never even heard of that word, nor of the Society for Psychical Research.

Mrs. Foster was impressed by Harold's grounding in the still-fledgling science. For his part, Harold was impressed by Mrs. Foster's powers. That was the basis for their friendship. Harold became a regular visitor to the cottage.

The widow had only one form of procedure: the Ouija board. This was a circle of polished wood twenty-seven inches across. Around the rim were the letters of the alphabet, placed out of rote. At one side was Yes, at the other side No. Sitters put their forefingers on an inverted cup, which was then expected to move to letters and spell out words.

Harold had read of the board in the SPR journal. He was able to tell Mrs. Foster that it was a progression of an earlier form called Planchette; that it had been a national craze in the United States in the twenties, now faded; that its name was simply a joining of the French and German words for the affirmative—*oui* and *ja*. What he refrained from telling was that he had always considered the Ouija board a mere parlour game.

It was more than that, he found out. With reservations.

Harold felt that when he and other sitters produced words and sentences on the board, the result was due, like dreams, to wishful thinking: the minds behind the fingers on the cup were unconsciously spelling out what they wanted to hear: forthcoming information was already known to the subliminal. But he was not positive. And this explanation failed when the board produced what sometimes turned out to be valid prognostications.

Harold's interest continued.

One night, he came home late from a seance. This sparked off an argument with Rosalind. All the couple's petty differences were brought up, and, inevitably, the subject turned to finance, in particular to the question of new curtains.

"We can't have them now," Harold said. "Impossible."

"You're always saying that."

"Well, I'll tell you something else we can't have this year."

"What?"

Harold sat down, the fire of his anger sinking. He had dreaded the moment when he would have to tell Rosalind there could be no holiday abroad this summer. He knew how much it meant to her.

He gave her the news. For a time she was silent, staring. Then she said in a bitter voice:

"If we're so damn poor, why don't we take in lodgers?"

Harold, tired of it all, said, "That's not a bad idea."

Rosalind left the room.

The next morning at breakfast, the sole exchange between the Lunns was Rosalind's "I'm going to put an item in the paper today" and Harold's "Fine. That back bedroom's just wasted space."

He left for work, feeling foolish. He wondered which of them had the less pride, which would be the first to call a halt. Later, however, in his office, he realised the idea could have good results. A boarder, some nice quiet lady, would be company for Rosalind as well as putting an end to her feeling of uselessness in the present crisis.

This was how the project seemed to develop. Although the boarder who eventually moved in was not quite what Harold had envisioned, everything else worked smoothly. Rosalind improved, became again the pleasant companion, the excellent wife. Also, the extra money was a distinct help with household finances. The boarder was unobtrusive, no trouble whatever.

So improved was Rosalind, in fact, that she accepted placidly Harold's announcement, early in 1937, that again there would be no foreign holiday this year.

Harold was content. Tranquility had returned to the domestic scene, his business worries were slowly but markedly easing, and in that third element of his life, the occult, there had been an interesting change of direction.

It had started with a conversation with Mrs. Foster. The subject was the anatomy of ghosts. Harold had retailed all the theories.

"I don't understand it," Mrs. Foster said. "And I don't know if I want to."

"You're not afraid of spirits, are you?"

"I think so, Mr. Lunn, yes."

"But what's the difference between a spirit who materialises and one who sends a message via the board?"

The sensitive shook her head. "We don't know where or who the messages come from. There's safety in doubt. In any case, the communications are good."

"And ghosts aren't, Mrs. Foster?"

"I don't know. But I can't see what good something does by flitting about in the dark. Ghosts could be evil, if they exist."

"I don't agree—about them being evil," Harold said. "About existence, that's something I'd love to investigate. But I don't know how to start."

"Spend a night in a haunted house."

"I would. Like a shot. If I knew where to find one."

Mrs. Foster said, "There's Gorse Manor."

Harold had known of Gorse Manor all his life. Not unusually, familiarity had blinded him to its significance. He had never paid much attention to the stories of short-term tenancies, of strange noises, of things seen in the grounds at night. They were all so fanciful.

He began to make enquiries. He talked to the woman caretaker who lived in the gatehouse. He had an interview with the agent in charge of the Gorse property. He sought out older people in the area who could give him the story without ninth-hand, third-generation embellishments. He wrote to South Africa to the present owner, a distant relative of the original James Gorse.

Harold got the key and permission to investigate. Both agent and relative were hopeful that he would make a negative report, enabling them to rent or sell the burdensome place.

One lunchtime, Harold went on a preliminary tour of the house, which he found uninspiring in aspect yet redolent with an atmosphere of waiting. It bode well. He was eager for the full moon, May 23, when he would sit up throughout the night in James Gorse's upstairs study.

———————◆———————

"Yes. That's all right."

Michael asked, "You didn't hear?"

"Very little."

"Good."

"You did well," Rosalind said.

"Yes."

"What a big old gloomy house."

Michael nodded. He lifted his hands from the chair and clasped them together on his stomach. Slowly, only his head moving, he began to look around the room.

The light from the half moon gave ample illumination. It glowed coldly on the furniture, on the vacant bookshelves, and on the large fireplace behind Rosalind—though the recesses on either side had mysterious shadows.

Michael's gaze around the room was not one of interest. It was an allaying ploy which would enable him to look at the door at his back without giving away his feelings.

He was still tense, still caught in the terror, like a fly at the edge of a web.

That figure he had seen downstairs, Michael thought. Was it hovering in the hall? Had it disappeared? Or was it moving slowly up the staircase? Was it gliding along the gallery? Was it, now, standing there in the open doorway?

Michael turned his whole body to look behind. The doorway was empty. A spasm ran through him and his back felt as though it were covered with ants.

The terror receded slightly.

But, Michael thought, the worst was yet to come.

Rosalind asked, "Michael?"

He turned. "Yes?"

"I see you're wearing the gloves. Good."

"I didn't forget," he said, still speaking in a whisper.

"You put them on outside? Out on the road?"

"Yes."

"And the bicycle?"

"Hidden in the grass."

"All correct," Rosalind said. The words and her voice were firm. She might have been a teacher talking to a student.

Michael whispered, "I didn't forget anything."

"You have a good memory."

"Yes," he said. "Yes."

* * *

When Michael Shield was five years old, his mother died. The reason for her absence from home was explained as a holiday. The real reason came some weeks later, as Michael and his father were talking by the fire one evening.

Mr. Shield said, with an odd curtness in his voice, "Mummy isn't coming back any more."

Michael was kneeling at his father's feet with a toy. He looked up and asked, "Why?"

"Because she's gone to heaven."

To his own surprise, Michael snapped, "You're a liar."

Mr. Shield's reaction was equally as abrupt and self-astounding: he slapped the boy's face.

The next moment they were in each other's arms, both sobbing. For that brief time, Michael felt curiously happy.

His longing for his mother was strong, once he knew the truth. He carried a remorseless ache. It was as if he had a weighty object inside his chest. Crying was good: it put helpful fingers beneath the weight; for a time. Another help, sometimes as strong as a pair of hands, was the pretence that his mother would soon be back from, variously, her season as a trapeze artist in a circus, a visit to a castle, her trip to America to see the cowboys. Predictably, Michael reverted to bed-wetting.

The Shield home was a detached house in a North London suburb. Mr. Shield held a high post with the London, Midland and Scottish Railway. An easy-going man with the warm smile of a young minister, he mourned so deeply and violently, and therefore therapeutically, over his marital loss that he was able to make a total recovery within six months. In another six months, he married again.

Penelope, as Michael was encouraged to call his step-mother, had a buxom and upright body and a pleasant, open face. She was a jolly person. She laughed often. Even when she wasn't smiling, her keen blue eyes seemed to be doing so.

Michael was soon able to convince himself that Penelope was his real mother; that she had come back after having a mysterious operation which had changed her appearance. In any case, as the months passed, time and the constant presence of Penelope combined to dim the original's image.

Yes, Penelope was his mother. And Michael grew worried. His bed-wetting, which had been sporadic during the early days of the new marriage, once again became regular.

It was not because of his feelings for Penelope. He neither loved nor disliked his stepmother. She aroused in him respect for her competence, admiration for her physical attractiveness, satisfaction that she was his mother and protector.

It was not because of Penelope's feelings for Michael, and her resultant treatment of him. She liked the boy well enough, found him reasonably self-sufficient and well-behaved, enjoyed buying him clothes and being seen with him—it gave her a pleasant feeling. She treated him with polite friendliness.

The trouble lay in the parental relationship. Mr. and Mrs. Shield were ill-matched. Not violently so. Theirs was not a mingling of incompatibles, of black and white, but of two shades of grey which were so alike they jarred.

What to many people appeared a laughably minute difference in personalities was actually a barrier of considerable height. Although hate and infidelity and ridicule could bring a marriage low, it could be brought even lower by what seemed in comparison to be innocent: boredom, incessant annoyance, disagreement. The first, at least, had its peaks to balance its nadirs. The second was a continuing middle-level of aggravation; a drain.

More relationships flounder on a running sea of trivia than

in a storm, just as a series of minor difficulties has greater de-
structive potential to the peace of mind than a tragedy.

Michael's parents bickered without end. The subjects of
strife ranged ludicrously from Penelope's refusal to buy eggs
unless they had brown shells to her husband's habit of replac-
ing books out of alphabetical order; more seriously from her
choice of friends to his choice of radio programmes; dan-
gerously from her love of the open air to his desire for the
hearth. They even bickered over the fact that each at times
refused to argue.

Penelope never turned her irritations on Michael. Having a
horror of being the stepmother of fictional tradition, she was
ever kind, if distant.

Nevertheless, Michael worried. He was apprehensive of his
mother's second departure. When it eventually happened, he
was frantic.

Although Penelope went home to her mother for only one
night, it set a precedent. Thereafter, she made the ten-mile
journey regularly and stayed away between two days and a
week. Her husband, too, as a form of self-defence, developed
the habit of leaving home for short periods, sleeping at his
club.

Michael lived in a perpetual state of anxiety.

During the longer periods of separation, he was sent to the
next suburb to stay with an aunt, his father's older sister. A
spinster, Aunt Maude was a sturdily built woman with a
round plain face and traces of a moustache. Her greying hair
she wore in a bun by day and put into pigtails for sleeping.
She dressed in blue serge suits and shoes as heavy as a hiker's.

Aunt Maude had a brisk manner. She was firm and forth-
right. The heartiness which sometimes appeared in order to
soften her approach had an uncomfortable air. Affection she
demonstrated with gruff, teasing compliments.

She felt duty-bound to like her nephew but was not going
to stand any nonsense. His infractions of her rigid household

rules were punished by verbal abuse, a barked gush of insult and threat and scorn.

Michael was happy at his aunt's. When there, he rarely wet the bed.

Occasionally, when newly arrived from home and still laden with his anxiety, he would deliberately break a rule so that he might be shouted at, thereby getting an immediate feeling of warmth and security.

Aunt Maude never used physical punishment, which was fortunate for Michael. Violence, even when unconnected with himself, made him nauseous.

At home, he was not aware of the fact that he sometimes introduced irksome topics or in other ways initiated friction, this in periods of domestic serenity.

Once he overheard a conversation between his stepmother and his aunt. Penelope said:

"I've been very lucky, of course. He's a quiet child. I could have found myself with an awful brat on my hands."

"True."

"Everything would be fine if he could only learn to control his bladder at night."

"Really? With me, he's made a mistake only once or twice."

"That's curious."

Aunt Maude said, "It's his little efforts at naughtiness that tax my patience."

"But he's never naughty at home. Never."

The two women agreed that Michael was an odd child; very odd.

Michael felt the same. He was not popular at any of the schools he went to over the years—Penelope changed her scholastic enthusiasms often. He refused to fight or join in the rougher games. Due to constant change and periods away at Aunt Maude's, he was a poor student. At twelve, he was learning with ten-year-olds. He built not one firm friendship.

He tended to incline toward the verbal bullies and the more sarcastic teachers. His greatest pleasure was reading.

Michael's height and bulk were increasing rapidly. He hated his size. Somehow, he managed to force on himself the belief that he was small and puny. He developed the habit of semi-crouching, like a beggar who lacks a deformity. In thought, he referred to himself as Little Ben, which was the name of his favourite comic-strip character, a rabbit who was the butt of all his animal friends.

At fourteen, further education seeming pointless, Michael was found a job in the left-luggage office of the local railway station. This was a disappointment to Mr. Shield, as well as embarrassing, but he didn't know what else to do with the boy, who had no interests and no goals and a feeble school record.

Michael was unconcernedly content with his work. Home life was much as before but he spent weekends at his aunt's. Pride had forced him to near-control over his bed-wetting.

Tardily, when fifteen and almost fully grown, Michael began to feel the stirrings of sexuality. His anxiety increased by his not knowing how to express himself in this new and disturbing direction. He was fully cognizant of the facts of sexual intercourse, and considered the act to be unpleasant, animalistic, and messy, like post-culinary functions.

He got little pleasure out of looking at the dirty pictures his work mates coveted, and he found their jokes disgusting. He didn't mind when they jeered at him. His preferred company was that of the girls who served in the refreshment room. Though they were cool to him, their talk was not so crude, more romantic than bestial. There were one or two he wouldn't have minded holding hands with, or even kissing, but he was too shy to make overtures.

The dreams which prefaced his occasional nocturnal emissions were peculiarly non-erotic, or so it seemed to Michael. In them he would be sitting within a circle of laughing girls, or being ordered out of a shop under the caustic eyes of staring customers, or kneeling before a stern matron, who was dressed in a quasi-military uniform, and accepting meekly her vilification of him.

The dreams he indulged in by day, his fantasies, were of wilder stuff, extensions of the others while owning more subtlety. Rarely did he see his imagined self through youth's customary trials leading to heroics. He was never a hero; always the scapegoat.

One daydream, which sent all others away to bemoan their weakness, came from his reading. The book was a detective story, the procedural type. He read the novel three times, always experiencing a wonderful tingling sensation during the final quarter.

The fantasy, or ambition, he turned to often thereafter, but generally on special occasions, feeling it was too precious to squander. He went on living this dread despite knowing that, because of his pacifistic personality, it could never come to be. That mystery novel changed Michael's life.

In his nightmares, he was always alone in darkness and trying to escape from that state into the crowd of people whose presence he could sense just around a corner.

One evening when Michael was seventeen, he came home from work to find the house full of people. Some he dimly recognised as relatives. His aunt was also there. Everyone had a stark-faced grimness which sent through Michael a not unpleasant shiver.

He was taken into the front room by Aunt Maude. She said, "Darling, you must be brave." Never before had she used an endearment.

While he knew that one or the other of his parents must be dead, it was Aunt Maude's top lip Michael was thinking of and looking at. The moustache was much denser nowadays.

She began to talk quickly, her usual calm gone. Michael gathered that the car had skidded, they had hit a tree, they had not suffered.

Michael wondered why she didn't shave. Several seconds

passed before he realised that the loud, toneless, continuing yell was coming from himself; that he was crouching with both hands over his ears, staring at Aunt Maude's hairy lip and keening out of a smiling mouth.

The door flew open, people rushed in, and Michael fainted.

A wretched five days preceded the funeral. The house, all its curtains drawn, was a dreary place full of whispers and women who made endless pots of tea. Every day saw a dozen callers—police, friends, a tailor, railway officials, the funeral director, solicitors, caterers. Everyone was dealt with efficiently by Aunt Maude.

When they were alone together at night, she and Michael played dominoes. Once he protested. He said, "I won't play." The rebellion was not met in the way expected. Instead of a stern rebuke, his aunt returned a kindly, "Whatever you say, darling."

Michael sagged. He said, "All right, I'll play."

For the funeral, every article of external clothing he wore was black except his shirt. Additionally, there were black ribbons on the lapel and sleeve of jacket and overcoat. Aunt Maude's veil reached her chest.

From the house, where the two coffins had been resting, open, on chairs in the front room, the motorcade went to the church. From there they went to the cemetery, from there to a restaurant. Michael, weary of the rites, ate quickly and slipped away.

He walked. He walked for hours. In him he felt an odd tingling. It was a more mature version of that which had beset him at intervals over the past days of wretchedness. He was both frightened and intrigued by the sensation. He mused that it might be a nervous reaction to the tragedy.

Twilight was approaching when he turned into a park. The tingling had grown now to a strident, insistent pitch. Its source seemed to be in his lower stomach. He had stopped wondering at its reason. He had stopped wondering about anything.

His head felt light, almost a separate entity, the way it had been when he had drunk wine once at a party. He was no longer intrigued or afraid. He was watching without emotion a young man in black walk the tarmac paths of a park.

He saw him stare keenly, though covertly, at everyone he passed. Little Ben seemed to be looking for something special or somebody in particular. His eyes were bright, there was a blotchy flush on his cheeks. He walked in a stoop more pronounced than the habitual. His movements were jerky.

Finally, away from the main path, he came to a slow halt near a bench. On it sat a woman. Middle-aged, she was neatly and dowdily dressed. There was no one else nearby. The woman was reading a newspaper.

Michael continued to stand there, some eight feet from the bench. The tingling was making him tremble. He saw everything with unusual clarity—the trees against the darkening sky, brown spots on the woman's hands, the untidy grass at the path edge, a discarded matchbox.

Repeatedly he glanced at the woman. Once when she looked up he quickly pretended to be intent on the branches high above. She went back to her newspaper. She had blue eyes and a mole on the farther cheek.

Dazed, trembling, feeling now a growing surprise, Michael heard himself pronounce one of the gutter words he had heard his work mates use.

Looking at the woman, he coughed to draw her attention, at the same time drawing back both sides of his coat.

The woman glanced up; started; stared.

Michael watched her hungrily. He ached with anticipation. His expression was eager, apologetic, and a little sad.

The woman's face had snapped to a dusky crimson. She was sitting stiffly upright. The newspaper, slipping from her hands, eddied gently to the ground.

Reason told Michael to run. Emotion ordered him to stay. He watched and waited.

Abruptly, the woman got to her feet. She held forward an

unsteady, threatening fist. Her other hand was clenched as if with fear. She began to stammer out words and unfinished sentences.

Beast. Should be locked. Filthy pig. Ought to be. Scum of the, scum of the. Beast. The Birch. That's what. Dirty animal.

Michael trembled and cringed and bathed himself in the vilification.

Growing wilder and even less coherent, the woman swung her head and called:

"Somebody! Somebody!"

Michael turned and ran.

Symbolically, he was starting on the path which would lead, a decade later, to a house in Stilton; the path which his mind had started to build when he was five years old, and which had been paved by his lovely daydream.

———————◆———————

Rosalind said, "Michael?"

He turned from looking at the study doorway. "Yes?"

"I see you're wearing the gloves. Good."

"I didn't forget."

"You put them on outside?" Rosalind asked. "Out on the road?" She was still speaking in a normal tone, declining the suggestion implied in Michael's whisper. She wondered when his tension was going to ease.

"Yes," he said.

"And the bicycle?"

"Hidden in the grass."

"All correct."

"I didn't forget anything."

Rosalind nodded. "You have a good memory."

"Yes," he said. "Yes."

Rosalind put her hands deeper in the pockets of her white raincoat. Briefly, she tightened her body. She felt chilled. Furthermore she was uncomfortable, standing here in the dreary room.

She said, "You obviously found the key without any trouble."

"Oh yes."

"That's not a part of it, of course."

"No," he said. "It doesn't matter."

Rosalind looked around, glanced at the window. She asked, "Which way did you come?"

"From town?"

"No, here. You know, from the trees."

"Across the lawn."

"That's what I thought," Rosalind said. "It came to me while I was waiting that it might be better if you circled it. Going straight across, you could be seen."

"I suppose I could, yes."

"Try and remember that, Michael. Circle the lawn."

"I'll remember."

Rosalind smiled, satisfied. She pressed her pocketed hands against her thighs in a mild shudder of self-love and anticipation.

Soon, she thought. It would be soon.

———◆———

When, in reply to her newspaper advertisement, Rosalind received via the box number a letter signed by an M. Shield, her only thought was that the name sounded solid and respectable.

It had not occurred to her that a man might answer—though there had been no mention of gender in the item which offered a furnished bed-sitting room and full board.

She wrote, asking M. Shield to call at Piper Street.

The next afternoon the doorbell rang. The visitor was a tall, stooping man about her own age. His clothes were new and of good quality, yet ill-fitting. His face, pale and plump, was noticeable only for its attractive eyes.

"Mrs. Lunn?" he asked shyly. He was standing semi-sideways, as though in readiness for a quick departure.

"Yes. Good afternoon."

"Good afternoon. I'm Michael Shield. It's about the room. You asked me to call and see it."

Rosalind began to nod slowly. She could say the vacancy had been filled, she thought. Admitting she wanted a woman boarder would make her look silly, in view of the advertisement.

Then Rosalind was struck by the idea that here she could score a greater triumph over Harold. Another man in the house, she mused, that would really give him something to fret about. He would insist they could manage without a boarder, and to prove it open up the purse-strings. It would have happened anyway, but would be swifter and more forceful with a man. She would have scored off Harold beautifully.

"Do come in, Mr. Shield," she said.

She showed him the room and the house. To everything he said a polite, "Very nice."

In the lounge she asked him to sit down, offered him a sherry, which he declined, and a cigarette, also declined, and said:

"What business are you in, Mr. Shield?"

"Well, none. I have private means."

"Where are you living at present?"

"In a hotel."

"Are you single?"

"Yes."

Rosalind could think of no further questions. There was a short, awkward silence before Michael Shield spoke.

He said, "I'll take the room, if that's all right."

She smiled. "You didn't ask how much it is."

"Oh yes. How much is it?"

She told him. He nodded, got out a checkbook, and paid for a month in advance. Five minutes later he left to fetch his cases.

Amused, Rosalind went into the kitchen to prepare the evening meal. She told herself that this was going to mean a lot of extra work. But she didn't mind. She felt sure it would be only for a few weeks. Harold would soon capitulate.

Later, when her husband came home, she said, "Our paying guest moved in."

Harold pecked her on the cheek. "Really?"

"*Mister* Shield."

He stood back and looked at her. "Well, well."

"He's young, good-looking, and presentable, and has a private income."

"That's interesting," Harold said, turning away to take off his coat. "What's for dinner?"

Obviously, Rosalind mused, the battle was not going to be won easily. Harold intended putting up a strong fight. It was a case of who would give in first; she because of the work and intrusion, Harold because of jealousy and having his pride hurt by neighbours' sniggers at the come-down. Her ground was the safest.

The weeks passed. Michael Shield stayed on. Neither Rosalind nor Harold voiced complaints. For Rosalind's part, her determination to hold out slackened, and in time was forgotten, as she became accustomed to the newcomer, as the work he caused was absorbed by existing chores, as the rent he paid eased the way and made possible many little treats.

After three months, the boarder was a permanent fixture.

Rosalind and Michael soon relaxed to first-name terms. They spent a good deal of time together. Most days, Michael would join her downstairs for morning coffee and for afternoon tea, going to his room when Harold was due from the office. After supper, he sometimes stayed on with the couple. He always stayed on if Harold went out.

Michael seemed to have no life outside the house. He read, went early to bed. He took walks in the neighbourhood almost every day when the weather was fine, and into town at weekends. Occasionally he went to the cinema.

In his long talks with Rosalind, he was open about his life except for a period of roughly three years, that between the

age of twenty-two and his arrival recently in Stilton. This intrigued Rosalind so much that she didn't press for details. She
formed, and then discarded, the suspicion that he had spent
that time in prison. She later decided he had been abroad
doing something brave and exotic and mysterious.

She liked Michael. He made her feel unusually mature.
That her liking was turning into a romantic fondness she
failed to realise until, one evening, the subject of ages came
up.

"I'm twenty-six," Michael said.

Rosalind lied, "So am I."

That was in the autumn of 1936.

Enthralled by this unexpected development in her life,
Rosalind romanticised the situation. She didn't see the sordid
aspect, the perennial dirty joke of wife and lodger; she was
protected by her cloak of specialness.

Her first impression of Michael she was able to eradicate
from her mind. He was handsome and strong, not, as she had
earlier said in an affectionate moment to Harold, "A nice
boy. A big plain softy."

Rosalind was happier, more particular about her appearance and her cooking, more attentive to her husband, doubly
efficient in the home. She sparkled.

Her relationship with Michael continued seemly. There
was no hint of familiarity, no double meaning in their talk.
They might have been siblings.

In Rosalind's feelings toward her paying guest there was
little of the carnal. She had no urgent desire to consummate
their relationship, was content with the living, throbbing lull.

Nevertheless, her fondness grew stronger. She convinced
herself that Michael had a fascinating background, that he
was in love with her, that if she were single he would declare
himself and whisk her off into an exciting life.

The Christmas holidays came. The Lunns were invited to
the usual parties. To some, they took Michael. He was not a
vivacious guest. He drank sparingly and joined in games

only with reluctance. Rosalind was disappointed that she could get no party kisses from Michael—though she appreciated his caution. To make up for it she flirted with other men while pretending they were her boarder.

The situation was unchanged until early February.

Then, Harold told Rosalind that again this summer they would be unable to take a holiday. She accepted the news with outward equanimity.

The next evening, Harold went to one of his regular meetings with Mrs. Foster, the spiritualist. He would not be back until late, Rosalind knew. She said blandly to Michael, who was sitting with her downstairs:

"Would you go to your room, please, and wait for me there. I have something to show you."

Michael went. Rosalind followed up the stairs five minutes later. Her mind empty, she entered her bedroom and stripped naked. She put on a robe. She went to Michael's room, tapped, and slipped inside.

He was sitting on the edge of the bed. Slowly he got up, looking at her in surprise. She drew open the front of her robe, revealing herself.

A curious expression crossed Michael's face. Rosalind interpreted it as wonder and desire. Letting the robe fall to the floor, she switched off the light.

For a moment all was black. Then faint light filtered into the room from street-lamps. Rosalind moved to where Michael stood.

"Quickly," she whispered. "Get undressed."

There was no response. He was like a sleepwalker. Rosalind understood: he could not believe that this was happening, that his dream of possessing his love was finally coming true.

Shivering now with the cold, she began to take off his jacket. He maintained his immobility. Jacket tossed aside, Rosalind unbuttoned his shirt.

"Quickly," she said. "It's all right. Honestly."

Michael started to fumble with his clothes.

Rosalind got into bed. She felt not sensuous but triumphant. She wouldn't have minded if it were all over and she were back in her own room.

She felt differently when Michael slipped into bed beside her. Pressing close to his nakedness, she was aroused by the youth and vibrancy which Harold lacked, stirred by the tense excitement she could sense in Michael, touched by his unsteady breathing and the pounding of his heart.

Further, she had a marvellous sensation of power, knowing that of the two loves, his was the deeper.

She began to kiss and caress him. She guided his hands. His tenderness was so pronounced it might have been mistaken, by a less understanding woman, for inexperience.

The act progressed to its logical end.

Giving Michael a final, gentle kiss on the brow, Rosalind eased herself from the embrace and got out of bed. She wanted to be alone in order to fully savour her power and triumph, hug herself in glee. She left the room.

From beginning to last, Michael had not uttered a word.

The next day, Rosalind was particularly nice to Harold, which heightened her pleasure. With Michael, when they were alone, she was affectionate and flirtatious. He did not respond. Irked and puzzled at first, she soon realised how sensible he was being: they could get used to the by-play and thoughtlessly slip into it when Harold was present. She returned to the friendliness of pre-consummation.

On an average of twice a week, Rosalind went into Michael's room for lovemaking. Sometimes during the afternoon she would take his hand and lead him upstairs. His response was always the same, and Rosalind never failed to be aroused. Michael became important to her.

Now she stayed on in bed with him when their passion was spent. They talked. More accurately, Rosalind talked and Michael made appropriate murmurs.

To him she poured out her desires for excitement and

travel—for, in fact, everything which she was convinced belonged to him. Not at any time did they discuss their affair and where it might lead. In the privacy of her own mind, however, Rosalind planned adventures abroad in company with Michael, who had become her passport to freedom, and somehow managed to believe that Michael was thinking in the same terms, just as she believed, in swift succession, that there would never be any more holidays with Harold, that she was destined to spend her life in suburban housebound drudgery, and that her husband was seriously ill.

Rosalind needed no evidence for her convictions. They were upturned pyramids balancing on a wish.

When she and Michael had been lovers for two months, Rosalind whispered to him in bed one evening, knowing he would understand:

"We can only do it, of course, if Harold dies."

———◆———

After glancing at the window, she asked, "Which way did you come?"

"From town?"

"No, here. You know, from the trees."

"Across the lawn."

"That's what I thought. It came to me while I was waiting that it might be better if you circled it. Going straight across, you could be seen."

"I suppose I could, yes."

"Try and remember that, Michael. Circle the lawn."

"I'll remember."

Rosalind smiled.

Michael knew that smile. He had seen it often in light as dim as this. It meant satisfaction.

"That's everything then," Rosalind said.

"Yes."

"How do you feel about it?"

"Fine," Michael said. "I'm fine."

She tilted her head in a question. "You're tense, that's all. I can see you are."

"Nerves."

"You'll be all right."

"Of course."

She nodded; then blinked; then nodded again. "The hammer."

"Yes."

"You didn't forget it?"

Michael reached into his inside breast pocket. He eased out from the tightness a short heavy hammer, the handle six inches long, the head a sledge-style, a simple block of iron.

Michael held the hammer out in his gloved hand. Rosalind looked away, saying, "Good." Michael let his hand droop to his side.

He tried not to think about it. Tried and failed. His tension was growing. There were aches in his legs from fighting the trembling there during the five minutes he had been here in this room.

Michael tried a diverting tactic with his tension, a switch of causes, which might make the effect easier to bear. He thought not of what lay ahead, but of that—that thing downstairs. The shape he had seen. The figure that might even now be hovering near the room's open doorway.

Michael shuddered. But terror was preferable to horror.

———◆———

"Yes. That's all right."

The voice belonged to Rosalind. Harold Lunn listened carefully. After a pause his wife said:

"Very little."

And, "You did well."

And, "What a big old gloomy house."

In between came low murmurs from a male voice.

The insanity of the situation suddenly occurred to Harold.

A look of bewilderment and disgust moved over his long face. He also felt ashamed of himself for this spying.

Leaving the foot of the stairs, he went softly back into the room where he had waited earlier. Again he brought into his mind the man he had seen briefly, two minutes ago, when moving into the doorframe. He remembered the darkling shape clearly, yet there was nothing he recognised.

Harold stood in the room, his head down, his body limp. He was in spiritual pain. He was caught between the desire to be far away from here, and the raving need to rush upstairs and burst into the study. He wanted to know why. He wanted to know who. He wanted to be mistaken.

It could all still have another meaning, he thought, lifting his head.

Three weeks before, Harold had attended a seance at Mrs. Foster's. There was only one other person present in the tidy parlour, a middle-aged widow who attended regularly in the hopes of receiving a message from her dead husband.

Harold was not attentive. While holding his finger on the upturned glass, he allowed his mind to wander to Gorse Manor. Arrangements had been concluded, he had been given a key to the house. He would go there in a month, when the moon was full.

After the seance, Harold stayed on for a cup of cocoa with Mrs. Foster. Pensively she said, "That was odd, I thought."

"What was?"

"The board spelling *Diary* like that, twice in a row. Does it have any meaning for you, Mr. Lunn?"

"I'm afraid not," Harold said. "And to be honest, I was thinking of something else at the time."

"Perhaps it means something for Mrs. Wales."

Four nights later, Harold attended another Ouija board session. Also there were a young couple. As soon as the sitters placed their forefingers on the cup, it began moving—unusually, since the norm was a certain amount of hesitant circling and jerking before direct action.

The cup spelled out *Diary*.

Then the seance continued, more or less successfully, the board producing little that was coherent.

Returning to the parlour from showing the couple out, Mrs. Foster said grumpily, "They weren't serious, those two. They were fighting to stop from giggling half the time. I won't let them come again."

Harold asked, "Did you note *Diary?*"

Her expression changed. "Yes. Very interesting. I had someone here last night and it didn't happen. The word must be for you."

"Mrs. Foster, do you feel up to another session?"

For an answer, she went to the table on which the board rested. Harold joined her. After sitting for a moment in silence, they reached out and placed their fingers on the glass. It dithered, then started to slide.

It went directly to D, next to I, next to A. . . .

After Y, the glass stopped moving.

Harold brought back his arm. He put his hands together in a steeple and smiled his intriguement.

"The message could, of course, be for you," he said.

Mrs. Foster shook her head. "I've thought and thought about it. I don't keep a diary. I don't know anyone who does."

"Nor I. My father had one. He called it his commonplace book. I burned it after he died."

"There might be some connexion there. Could your father be trying to tell you something?"

"I don't know," Harold said.

Driving home, he remembered that he did know someone who kept a diary—his wife. Rosalind as a diarist, however, was far from diligent; she went for months without writing a word. Harold discarded that possibility and went back to thinking about his father.

Two mornings later, getting a clean shirt from a chest of drawers in the bedroom, Harold noticed with surprise that the position of the Gorse Manor key was different.

The black, rusting piece of metal had been at the side of the drawer when he had last seen it; now it lay in the corner. There was no apparent reason for the change, no article of clothing having been added or removed.

Harold was troubled as well as intrigued. The lower half of the chest belonged to Rosalind. In the bottom drawer was her diary.

Surely, Harold thought, there had to be some significance in this. As coincidence it was too startling. So, the answer was simple: ask Rosalind what she had been putting in her journal lately.

But while he was dressing, it occurred to Harold that his wife might not want him to be privy to her writings, that the point of the Ouija-board message was that the diary held an important fact which he would not learn through Rosalind.

She could be in some sort of trouble, he mused. She could be ill. Perhaps she had done something criminal. She might have got herself into debt. There were many motives for secrecy, and for her need of help.

At breakfast, Harold made no mention of the diary.

Throughout the day he pondered the problem. Reading his wife's private journal without her permission was immoral. On the other hand, not to read it in this particular instance could be disastrous.

He reached a decision while driving home.

After greeting Rosalind with the usual kiss on the cheek, Harold went upstairs to wash. He closed the bedroom door, crossed to the chest, and pulled open its bottom drawer. His heart was beating at an alarming speed.

He got out the diary. For the first few days of the new year, the pages were full—parties, resolutions, everyday occurrences. Many blanks followed, with the occasional burst of writing activity, each one on routine matters. After another blank stretch came the single line *He is crazy about me.*

Harold's body tensed. His heart, which had been settling,

returned to its rapid drum. Refusing to think beyond the line, he went on turning pages.

Washed hair.

Blank and two pages of recipes.

Wrote to Mummy.

He's a wonderful person.

Blank.

I'd like to make the first move but I haven't the nerve.

Good film at the Rialto.

It's in his eyes when he looks at me.

Blank.

No holiday this year.

We are lovers!

Harold felt weak. His arms sagged. He was dizzy and sick. That his wife was having a love affair was the last thing he had expected, and the worst he could imagine. He loved Rosalind.

Too shattered to read on, he put the diary away and lay on the bed.

It was only natural that the first person who came under his suspicion as the lover was Michael Shield. But he couldn't accept that, couldn't believe Rosalind would be attracted to the bumbling young man. It had to be someone else.

Quickly, he got off the bed and retrieved the diary. He flipped through the pages up to the present. The entries were all short and none gave a name.

The last entry, three days before, said, *Everything's settled. We go there on the sixteenth.*

Harold thought this must mean she and the lover were planning a rendezvous. Which definitely ruled out Michael Shield as the man, for they had ample opportunities at home without having to go elsewhere.

It could also mean the relationship was not yet sexual. *Lover* did not necessarily signify intimacy. Perhaps there was still hope.

"Harold!"

It was Rosalind calling from downstairs.

He put the diary away, forced himself to an appearance of normalcy, and left the room.

Harold performed his act over the following two weeks. He watched his wife closely, seeing nothing amiss. He read her diary every morning and found there no name. He checked the position of the key, saw it hadn't changed, and for safety put it in his wallet. He attended a seance at Mrs. Foster's but received no message, nor was there a repeat of *Diary;* in that respect, when questioned by the medium, he said it must have been to do with his father's commonplace book.

The evening of May 16, Harold was due to go to Mrs. Foster's. He left the house at dusk, drove to the end of Piper Street, and parked around the corner. Getting out, he stood where he could see his house in the distance.

Presently, Rosalind appeared. She turned in Harold's direction. He returned to the car, which stood in dimness between lamp-posts.

Waiting, he felt relief at the fact that his wife was not carrying a case: he had suspected all along that the sixteenth was the night of a final departure.

Rosalind passed the junction. Circumspectly, Harold followed in the car. His wife was headed out of town, it seemed. Soon she left an outer suburb and the last of the street lighting.

Harold parked the car and continued on foot, as his lights would make his slow presence known. He had no trouble keeping Rosalind in view. Her white raincoat gleamed in the darkness.

They were on the road which led past Gorse Manor. Harold was thinking how odd it would be if they had chosen . . . When Rosalind turned in at the gateway of the estate.

Puzzled, he followed, moving silently past the gatehouse. He stepped onto the driveway's edging of grass. He felt chilled and strange and desperate.

At the front of Gorse Manor, Rosalind moved up under the portico. A moment later she went inside the house.

Harold stopped. He got out his wallet. The Gorse key was still there. How had she got in the house? he wondered. Had her lover let her in, having himself made a forced entry?

Another question brought a tingle to the hairs on the nape of his neck:

Was her nameless lover flesh and blood?

Harold took the key from his wallet and went on. Using great stealth, he let himself into the house. Light from the half moon illuminated the interior.

Pausing on the threshold, he heard a sound of movement from upstairs; from James Gorse's study. After that—silence.

Harold moved across the hall slowly. He stopped at the stairfoot. There was still no sound from above.

Irresolute, confused, and wondering if he were under observation, Harold moved to the nearest doorway and into a butler's pantry. For ten minutes he stood gazing at the empty shelves, trying to decide on a plan of action.

He heard, or thought he heard, a faint sound from the direction of the main entrance. He listened for a moment before moving to the doorframe.

He saw a man. The man was crossing the hall. He stopped —and Harold withdrew, stepping back into the pantry while still facing the door. He saw the man go past and crept forward again. A minute later, from upstairs, he heard Rosalind say:

"Yes. That's all right."

Now Harold was standing limply, depleted and in emotional pain. He had made an attempt at telling himself the whole thing could have another meaning, be a mistake, that he was putting a wrong construction on words and events. Useless. Rosalind was obviously having an affair with the man, and that truth might as well be accepted.

So what now? Should he rush upstairs?

Harold shrank from such an action. It was anathema to his

character. He didn't fear the lover, he simply loathed the thought of the scene with its naked emotions, the thought of the shock to Rosalind followed by her hatred of him and shame for herself.

Besides, Harold mused, a confrontation could force the couple into a course they otherwise might not take. If left alone, allowed to work out their passion, it could well be that the affair would die.

Harold liked that idea. From it he drew strength and comparative calm. He reminded himself that he and Rosalind and the lover were living an old, old story, a tale so trite it hardly raised an eyebrow on the listener who was out of the triangle. Only once out of ten times did the story end in divorce. The watchword was patience.

Meanwhile, Harold thought, he would continue his act of ignorance, carry on just as usual with his life and routine. He would even go now to Mrs. Foster's, and would come here as planned on the twenty-third. With Rosalind he would be kinder and more attentive (he may, unknowingly, have been neglecting her these past months) and allow her extra money for her vanities. It would all work out.

Mouth firm, eyes sad, Harold left the room.

"How do you feel about it?" Rosalind asked.

"Fine," he said. "I'm fine."

"You're tense, that's all. I can see you are."

"Nerves."

"You'll be all right."

"Of course."

Rosalind said, "The hammer."

"Yes."

"You didn't forget it?"

Michael reached inside his jacket. Rosalind watched his movements carefully. They seemed sure enough, steady. She watched until his gloved hand reappeared, now holding the hammer, when she looked away.

She said, "Good."

Still with her eyes averted, Rosalind checked over her mental list of essentials. There seemed to be so many. So many details to consider. Nothing must go wrong. There had to be no possibility of involvement. People wouldn't understand. They didn't know about Harold's sickness. Self-interest came into it, too, of course. But a lot of it was mercy. He could linger on and on. Better quickly than that.

Rosalind looked back at Michael sharply as from the boundary of her vision she saw him make a small, sudden movement, like a start of surprise.

He was standing with his arms at his sides and his head turned away.

She asked, "What is it?"

Michael whispered, "Did you hear that?"

"No. What? I didn't hear anything."

"Listen," Michael hissed, shaking his head for silence. The sound, faint, had come from below. It had been like that of a door closing.

The seconds crawled by. There was nothing else to be heard. Michael told himself he had imagined the sound.

He could, he thought, be imagining the whole thing. This room, the house, Stilton, Piper Street, Rosalind. It was all too strange for reality. There had been other imaginings, equally as odd and complicated and drawn out. They had been more important than true living—or existence, for that was all it had been. Perhaps still was. Perhaps he was not here but sitting in reverie, soon to be jerked alert by the bell. If so, when he went back to his reverie afterwards, he would hurry it along and leap the horror. He wouldn't go back to the beginning.

Rosalind spoke, breaking into his thoughts. She asked, "What did you hear?"

Michael said, "Nothing."

--------◆--------

Living with the Lunns was like being in a sort of limbo, he found. It was more comfortable and less transient than staying at a hotel, yet without the permanency of a real home.

He had a feeling of waiting. He was living a pause. This gave him a certain amount of satisfaction, which, he considered, might be specious: after what lay behind, almost anything would be satisfying.

His room was cheerful, the house pleasant, the food excellent. Mrs. Lunn had a polite manner. Mr. Lunn's attitude was condescending, banter without the softening edge of friendliness.

Because he sensed she was in need of an ally, Michael responded to the offered camaraderie of Mrs. Lunn, who then became Rosalind. They spent much time together, talked warmly on a hundred subjects and about themselves.

To Michael, Rosalind was simply a sociable person. He found her not particularly interesting. He felt older than she in many ways, even though they were the same age. What he liked most about her was her prettiness.

As the months passed, Michael's suspicion regarding the speciousness of his satisfaction was proved correct. He began to get restless. He yearned for stability, order, control. The continuing limbo was unsettling, like walking an endless kerbstone. While anticipation may often be more pleasing than realisation, the latter has to happen to permit the comparison. All Michael's old anxieties were returning.

From time to time, Michael experienced a familiar tingling sensation. It frightened him. He countered his desire by engaging Rosalind in earnest conversation. The talk and her feminine presence helped. He always won the fight, though victory left him depressed and exhausted, as if he had expended great energy in a cause which had failed.

Mr. Lunn, with whom he stayed on formal-name terms,

remained the same as when Michael had first moved in. He was aloof and supercilious. Often at mealtimes he acted as though the boarder were not present. Michael scented resentment.

Rosalind, however, changed. Physically, she seemed to get more glamorous, neater, with never a blemish on her appearance. In manner she grew warmer, more outgoing. Michael would catch her looking at him with an odd expression in her eyes. She was conscious of her person, fluffing back her hair, swaying, moving with grace. Her attentiveness increased.

Michael would have called her attitude flirtatious, except for knowing that this was silly. Happily married women didn't go in for that sort of thing.

One evening, after Mr. Lunn had gone out, Rosalind said, "Would you go up to your room, please, and wait for me there. I have something to show you."

Puzzled, Michael obeyed. It occurred to him that Rosalind had been unusually reserved today. Ever since breakfast, when she had talked quietly of there being no holiday this year, she had seemed distant and disinclined to socialise, like someone whose thoughts were elsewhere.

Michael sat on his bed. Presently, Rosalind came in. She was wearing a robe.

The following fifteen minutes was the most astounding period of Michael's life. It was a revelation, a riot of firsts. Never before had he seen a naked woman, or been kissed like that, or had his intimacy touched, or caressed the silk-smooth flesh of a female, or been allowed the ultimate.

Emotions jostled for prominence. Surprise at her state of dress gave way to shock at her sudden nudity. Closely following was a feeling like envy, which he didn't understand. Next came embarrassment, turning into pride at being desired, turning into annoyance at his bumbling over his getting undressed. One second later he was marvelling at how cool he was being in stripping off in such a sophisticated way. Disbelief had taken over by the time he got into bed.

For the rest, there were the dozens of emotions which go to make up that assumed single, pleasure.

Afterwards, Rosalind kissed his forehead and slipped away. He was glad. Being alone, he could work better at getting his thoughts in order. But continuing astonishment rendered cogitation difficult. It was yet another emotion which came instead of thought.

Michael felt guilty. It was the same as that which he used to feel after his verbal abuses. Now it was on account of Mr. Lunn. Michael told himself he was a traitor, a subversive. He had stolen. He had wounded. He had broken into the happiness of others.

It was in this mood that Michael eventually fell asleep.

The next day, Rosalind was coquettish. Not knowing how to react, having had no experience of this game, Michael stayed as before. He was relieved when Rosalind followed suit.

Their sex continued. Michael, trying to get the affair in perspective, wondered if this was the end of his limbo, the realisation he had been waiting for. He failed to see, however, where the association could lead. He was not in love with Rosalind. He still felt guilty about Mr. Lunn. He was more stricken with anxiety than ever.

Had Michael owned sufficient firmness of purpose, he would have left.

Rosalind, fortunately, never talked of what might lie ahead for them. After intimacy, her murmurous chatter was all of travel and far, exotic places.

One evening in bed, she was silent for a long time. Finally she said:

"We can only do it, of course, if Harold dies."

Michael was shocked. So shocked that he became an emotional vacuum.

He said, "Yes."

"It's the only way, dear."

"Yes."

"You do see that?"

"Of course."

Michael was only dimly aware of having spoken. He got out of bed, stepped to a chair, and sat down. Picking up his shirt from the floor, he held it on his lap. He began to fiddle with a button, looking at it closely. Shock slowly withdrew.

He was excited.

Looking up and around, Michael saw that Rosalind had gone. He stood up, the shirt falling unheeded, and strained his body to an elated tautness, a stalk reaching for the sun. He stared upward, mouth in a slack smile. His daydream was up there somewhere.

If only he could believe it were possible.

His excitement eased, his tension evaporated, he sat down and wept quietly.

The next afternoon he went into the kitchen and touched Rosalind's arm. He said, "Let's go to bed." It was the first time he had been the instigator.

They made love quickly, as if it were a chore which had to be put out of the way in order for enjoyment to thrive. Breaking their embrace, they lay side by side.

In a moment, Rosalind said, "He's a sick man."

Michael liked that. He wanted it. He asked for assurance. "Really ill?"

"Really ill. But he could linger. You know."

"Sad."

"I hate to see that sort of thing."

"Yes," Michael said. He added, for clarity, "Yes, I hate to see it as well."

There was a pause. Rosalind felt for Michael's hand, took it and squeezed. He squeezed back.

Rosalind murmured, "Something must be done."

"I agree."

"For us as well as Harold."

"Yes."

Nothing more was said then. But the pattern had been set.

Thereafter, Michael and Rosalind took up their dialogue whenever they were lying together in bed, in dimness, which became a daily event. Some days there was no sex. By silent, mutual agreement, the matter was discussed at no other time. They might spend two hours downstairs chatting about local politics, then go to Michael's room, strip, and get into bed, and begin on a terse, whispered exchange.

Michael was happier than at any time in his life. Realisation was on its way. He lived in a steady simmer of excitement. That his anxiety had not totally disappeared, held on there in low key, was due to the knowledge of what inevitably must be done.

It was two weeks before he and Rosalind reached that point in their furtive talks.

They had covered everything else: Harold's money (a small fortune), whether or not Rosalind would sell the house (yes), the first cruise they would take (Greek Islands), if Michael should move elsewhere for the time being (no).

Rosalind said, "It will have to look like an accident, of course."

"That's certain. That has to be."

"A car. Our car. Something could be done that way."

"I can't drive."

"I can. But I don't know if . . . You know."

"This is my work," Michael said. "I must be the one."

"Yes. You're strong. You're wonderful."

"What about a gun?"

"Where would we get one?"

"I don't know. And I've never fired a gun. I think I could do it though."

"In London. Some big city. You can buy anything in a big city."

"Yes."

Rosalind said, "But the noise. It would have to be somewhere miles from anywhere. Otherwise people would come quickly."

"There are lots of ways. Lots."

None, however, seemed to be right. As the days passed, Michael and Rosalind found method elusive when combined with opportunity. While Rosalind appeared to seethe quietly, Michael was undisturbed by the impasse. It was part of that delightful expectation.

They talked of suspicion. Should the death be seen as not an accident, would they be suspected? Michael insisted they would not. Rosalind seemed happy to agree.

One morning at the breakfast table, Harold announced his latest project in connexion with his occult interest. He looked proud and keen.

"It's taken quite a bit of arranging, I can tell you," he said. "Finally, everything's fixed. I get the key today. I'll do it on the twenty-third."

"Alone?" Rosalind asked.

"Absolutely."

Michael said, "Won't you be frightened, Mr. Lunn?"

"Ghosts don't hurt," Harold said scornfully. "That's for children to believe in. Ghosts, if there are any, are intangible."

His wife asked, "What will you do actually?"

"Simply sit in the study and wait. And hope."

Rosalind leaned forward. She was smiling, but Michael could tell that the smile was only on her lips. She asked:

"What will you do if you hear someone creeping up behind you?"

"Nothing. Nothing whatever."

"Truly?"

Harold nodded. "I'd be afraid of frightening the thing away. I'll be as still as a mouse."

Rosalind leaned back. Going on with her meal, she asked in a different tone, "Who owns that place now?"

When the front door closed behind Harold Rosalind and Michael exchanged glances, rose from the table, and left the room. They went upstairs, drew the curtains, undressed calmly, got into bed, and lay side by side.

Rosalind said, "May twenty-third."

"All right. How?"

"What we said before. The cleanest and quickest."

"Yes, a blow on the head."

"Now the opportunity's there. The place."

"It's perfect."

"You can do it?"

"I can."

"It will be seen as . . . as not an accident, naturally."

"But it won't matter."

"That's what I thought straightaway."

"They'll think it was something to do with the supernatural."

"Exactly."

"That's it then. The twenty-third. That's final."

"Darling," Rosalind said.

* * *

"What is it?"

"Did you hear that?"

"No. What? I didn't hear anything."

Michael shook his head and said, "Listen."

She watched him and listened. There was nothing to hear. This room, the house beyond, all was silent, as it had been all along. Only once, while waiting, had there been a noise, and that was the sound of a lorry in the distance.

Michael was nervous, Rosalind thought. If anything, he seemed to have more taut agitation now than when he had first come in the room.

She asked, "What did you hear?"

He turned back. "Nothing."

Rosalind gave him a smile of encouragement. She hoped it would convey that she had the utmost confidence in him, which was the truth. She knew he would implement the plan without flinching. There was great strength in Michael beneath the mild façade. The end he would accomplish, just as she had accomplished her own part of it.

Rosalind had been the planner. She it was who had strolled one afternoon around the back yard of an iron foundry, picking up small pieces of metal, one of which had been right for the key. She had chosen the small hardware shop on the other side of town where Michael had bought the file—also, on her instructions, several other articles so that the file purchase would not be remembered particularly. She had sat beside him as he worked at copying the original, taken from Harold's drawer. She had gone herself to Gorse Manor to make sure the copy turned the lock.

She had decided which of the hardware stalls on Stilton's street market would be best, and which time during Saturday afternoon would be busiest, and what size hammer Michael should buy, and that he should make only that one, fast purchase.

It was Rosalind who had planned this trial run, a full dress rehearsal for Michael, on an evening when Harold was safely out of the way at Mrs. Foster's. And it had worked beautifully.

"That's everything then," Rosalind said.

"I think so."

"Afterwards you go back exactly the way you came."

"Yes."

"I'll be waiting at home and we'll say we were together there all evening."

"Perfect," Michael said. He spoke in a hoarse whisper. His throat felt dry and tight. He was surprised that he was able to speak at all.

The horror was coming.

His breathing tightened.

The horror was now.

Rosalind said, "There aren't too many details really. There's not that much to confuse you, Michael."

She waited for him to answer. He did not. He stood there as before, arms at his sides.

Rosalind said, "Michael?"

Still no answer. And Rosalind saw now, moving her upper body forward slightly, that Michael was not giving her his attention.

He was looking past her, gazing at somewhere beyond her left shoulder.

She repeated his name, doing so with a firm edge on her voice.

No reaction.

His eyes seemed to be fixed on one spot. Rosalind judged it to be the alcove beside the chimney-piece. She felt the first inklings of alarm.

There was another factor: the atmosphere. It had changed. The room seemed quieter, stiller. But there was something else. Something strange.

"What's the matter, Michael?"

He licked his lips. They were trembling. His eyes were still fixed on the same spot.

"What's wrong?" Rosalind asked. Now she, too, was whispering. "You're frightening me."

He said nothing. Suddenly, his eyes grew wider.

Rosalind's heart lurched. Convulsively she clasped her hands together. Her back felt cold. She wanted to look around. She couldn't bring herself to do that. She stared at Michael.

"Darling," she said weakly. "Please."

His lips were moving. It seemed as though he wanted to say something but was having difficulty finding words. Rosalind strained forward, aching in her fear, and at last Michael spoke.

He said, "There's something behind you."

On the twenty-third of May, 1937, the moon was full. It hung in the clear night sky like a grapefruit ripe to bursting point. The town of Stilton was illuminated by the silvery glow to a mid-gloaming brightness.

The light had particularly good effect in the areas not served by street-lamps. One of these was a lane of terrace houses.

The facing rows of identical homes had their harshness of utility softened by the moonlight. They looked charming instead of stolidly respectable, warm instead of cold in apathy, quaint instead of grimly, determinedly characterless.

In front of one house stood a car. It was plain black and unmarked. Its parking lights were on, it had an air of waiting.

More than one curtain in the street had twitched as occupants sneaked looks at the vehicle, wondering if this nocturnal activity of Jack Cartland's spelled the latest development in the case all Stilton had been agog with over the past week.

Inside his house, Inspector Cartland was passing the time by washing the dishes from his supper.

The combination living room and kitchen had a rigorously tidy look. Neither flounce nor flower nor strewn garment broke the continuity of hard neatness. This had nothing to do with the street's ethos of the primacy of appearances, and less to do with the personality of Jack Cartland.

A widower of eight years, he spent as little time as possible in a house whose memories still caused him pain. He had no wish for it to have an enticing homeliness.

Standing at the sink, the inspector hummed as he worked. He always hummed when he was stimulated. Part of his arousal was due to the unorthodoxy of the experiment tonight. He had always been attracted to the off-beat, the line that wavered from officialdom's grain.

In the main, however, he was excited because of his hopes.

Jack Cartland was sixty-four years old. In five months he would retire as head of Stilton's CID, a division composed of four plain-clothes detectives. He had given his life to the police force; and he was glad. His thoughts had never run in any other direction.

Yet he did own a regret. It had been growing in him implacably like a tumour during the past half-dozen years. Sometimes he smiled it away. More often, especially when he was in his house, he welcomed the regret sadly. It had become something like a companion: disagreeable, given to wounding, caustic, but a companion nonetheless.

Jack Cartland wanted to put a crown on his career. He loved the idea of going out in a blaze of glory. Like all dogs, good or bad, he longed to have his day. He didn't want to sidle into retirement via a dinner at the town hall with all those awkward speeches and the presentation of a gold-plated watch, followed by a half-column review of his career in Stilton's *Evening News*.

That would come anyway, of course, though in much grander style, if he had his crown, his coup, his great big beautiful bonfire of celebrity which would light not only Stilton but the whole county.

Thus his regret. What hopes hereabouts of catching bank robbers, arresting a crooked financier, uncovering a nest of German spies? What use were shoplifters, wife-beaters, burglars, and car thieves?

The questions formed his defence. It was a reasonable brief which nevertheless always lost. Jack Cartland's regret had flourished.

His wish for a crown was not mere vanity, though that was there too. He knew his wife would have been proud of him, and, almost as important, that his two married daughters would feel less the drudgery of their lives.

His hope had shrivelled in ratio to the growth of his regret. He had accepted that the chances were delicately slender of his someday being indicated as "That's the man who . . ." rather than "Used to be a copper."

Then had come the morning of May 17.

Humming, Inspector Jack Cartland dried and put away the crockery from his meal of beans on toast. He hung the cloth on its hook. Turning, he looked about for what might need aligning and rendering lifeless.

Cartland was a tall and hefty man, ungainly. He had a swooping paunch like half a pear. His arms were long, his feet large, his hands as bloated and un-nimble as inflated rubber gloves.

His hair, mist-white, was short and shaved high above the ears. He had a broad face of craggy features which looked as if they had been put together out of smaller lumps. For a mouth he had an upcurling slice of thin space. His grey eyes, hooded with pouches of flesh, were kindly and mournful and whimsical.

He wore a tweed suit whose lapels curled like stale sandwiches. The knees were baggy. The waistcoat was open on the bottom three buttons to accommodate that paunch. His shirt was blue with a detachable white collar. His tie was grey; he owned a dozen ties and they were all grey; it was the midway stage between colour and mourning.

From his big black regulation boots to his cropped hair, Jack Cartland looked a policeman.

Satisfied with his chores, the inspector glanced at his watch and checked it with the clock on the mantel—a present to mark his thirtieth year on the force. The time was five minutes to ten.

Still humming, he switched off the light, fumbled his way along the dark hall, and went out to the car.

It had been quite a week, he thought. Quite a bloody week.

"Murder."

"What did you say?"

"That's right, Jack. It looks like a plain case of murder." The sergeant's voice came over the line as a thin quiver of excitement. It reached inside the inspector and found a mate.

"Sam, I'm only half awake. Say the word again."

"Murder."

"Okay."

"Better look lively, Jack."

"What time is it?" Cartland asked, pinching the bridge of his nose.

"Seven. I would've waited till eight but I knew you'd want to be told at once."

The inspector had been dragged from sleep by the ringing of the telephone. Eyes slitted, he had got up, put on the old overcoat which served as a robe, and gone out to the landing. Telling himself for the hundredth time he should get an extension installed in his bedroom, he had gone downstairs to the hall.

He straightened, took a tighter grip on the instrument, and turned his back on the daylight yelling through the door's upper panel of glass.

"All right, Sam," he said. "Start at the beginning."

"Last night it was. Eleven o'clock. Constable Pierce took the call. It was anonymous. The man said, 'There's a body in Gorse Manor.' Just that. Just those few words. He rang off and—"

"Hold on there," Jack Cartland said. "You're going too fast."

"Sorry."

"The telephone call. Was there anything distinctive about the man's voice? Tone, accent?"

"I don't know, Jack. I'll talk to Pierce about it."

"No. I will. What did the constable do?"

"Well, he thought it was probably some fool, or a bloke who'd had a pint too many and wanted to give the police a bit of a wild-goose chase. Anyway, we're always getting calls about that place—lights seen and figures moving about. That sort of nonsense."

"So he did nothing."

The sergeant's voice was persuasive. "You can't blame the lad, Jack. I'd have acted the same."

"Never mind," the inspector said. "Go on." Although he knew it would be better to get the story in person, not over the telephone, he couldn't wait.

His excitement, however, had remained at the same low pitch. The murder scene promised not the dramatic but the sordid. Gorse Manor, a so-called haunted house, had often been broken into. Jack Cartland thought the victim was probably some pathetic tramp, or a meths drinker who had been killed over ownership of a half bottle. But murder was murder, a rarity in Stilton.

"Any road," the sergeant said, "when I relieved Constable Pierce this morning at six, I sent him to have a look. The place was closed but he got a key, woke up the caretaker that lives in the gatehouse. A Mrs. Trent."

"What about her? Anything to say?"

"She knows nothing. Sleeps like a top."

"Okay. So Pierce went in the house."

"Yes," the sergeant said. "And true enough, there's this dead woman upstairs."

Cartland straightened a fraction more. "A woman?"

"That's right. Pierce phoned me from the gatehouse ten minutes ago, and I called you."

A female derelict, the inspector thought.

He said briskly, "Very good, Sergeant. Get things moving. Send Tarkinson with that fingerprint set of his. Also Dr. Patcher. Also that commercial photographer we used last year. Ask the hospital to be ready to send an ambulance. Do that, then get a car over here for me."

"Yes, sir."

Jack Cartland put the telephone back in its cradle. He stared at it for a moment before turning quickly away.

Fifteen minutes later, he was standing impatiently out on the street. He had cut his chin while shaving and had sealed the wound by sticking on it a piece of paper.

A searchlight of sun, evading the forest of chimneys, laid a yellow streak along the rooftop opposite. Cartland smiled tightly. He wondered why, since policemen hated murderers, they always got excited about murder.

The car came, a uniformed constable at the wheel. He said, as they drove off, "This might not be an easy one, sir."

"Why's that, son?"

"The woman. A glamorous bit of stuff, I understand."

Cartland looked at the young man. His inner chord of stimulation thrummed hopefully. He said, "Sam didn't mention that."

"Pierce told me just now when I drove Mr. Tarkinson out there. She's young and pretty and very well dressed."

"Is she indeed?"

"Yes, sir. A blonde."

The inspector turned back to stare at the road. Could this be it? he wondered. Could this be the coup, the blaze, the crown?

He told himself not to think about it. He watched the awakening town and nervously picked the paper off his cut.

When the car drew up in front of Gorse Manor's portico, a young, pink-faced constable came down the steps. He snapped a trembly salute, like a recruit meeting his first general.

"Good morning, sir."

"Hello, Pierce," the inspector said, getting out of the car. "I hope you didn't touch anything."

The constable's eyebrows were unsteady. "Oh no, sir."

"Any new developments?"

"Yes, sir. There's a basement window broken around the back there. It's right over the latch. Too well placed to be an accident."

"Footprints?"

"It's all concrete there."

"Well, we can ask the caretaker about that window."

Constable Pierce said, "I already did, sir. She says the break wasn't there a week ago."

The inspector lifted and dropped his shoulders. "Too bad she couldn't get closer than that. Still, it's something."

"Yes, sir."

"Any ideas about the anonymous caller?"

The constable shook his head like a friend over a coffin. "It was done so quick like. I've given it a lot of thought since, and I can't tell you anything except the words."

"All right, son," Cartland said. "You're doing fine." He went on and up the steps, thinking, Too bloody fine. They had to be watched, these eager young Pierces. They'd solve a case from right under your nose.

The door stood open. Its handle was coated with streaks of black powder. At the other end of a vast hall a staircase rose. By the foot of the stairs a man was bending over the balustrade.

He glanced around as Cartland approached. He was thirtyish, thin, and melancholy-looking, like the men who queued for the dole on Fridays.

Glumly he said, shaking a brush, "Nothing on the door and only smudges here so far. Good morning."

"Morning, Tarky. Where's the body?"

Detective Tarkinson pointed up to a gallery. "Last door. I haven't been in there yet."

"Good. Me first, doctor next, then you, then the photographer. Meanwhile, when you've finished here, have a go at the broken window Pierce found. He'll show you."

"Righto."

Jack Cartland went upstairs. He was breathing heavily when he reached the gallery, and was glad to be alone so he had no need to hide the gasps.

Vain old bastard, he thought.

The end room. He went in. His eyes were drawn at once to a figure in white.

The woman was lying in an alcove beside the fireplace, lying on her back with no more disarray of limbs than if she had been asleep.

Cartland stood beside her and bent from the waist. He noted the expensive raincoat and shoes, the wedding ring, the fact that her hair was dyed.

She was unusually pretty and well-groomed, he mused. She couldn't be more than twenty-five years old. They were there, all the attributes needed for a model, a singer, an actress, some celebrated . . .

The inspector felt ashamed of himself for his hopes, craving that glamorous touch or name which would lift the case to the headlines. A young life had been clicked off like a light and all he could think of was himself.

He lowered his bulk to one knee. "Sorry, kid," he said.

Her face was peaceful in death. The end had been fast. On her right temple, beside the hairline, was a mark, a slight indentation about the size of a matchbox. It smoothed up into the surface at one end.

Jack Cartland peered at it closely.

Crow-bar, he thought. Tyre-lever. Ornament with a square base. Stonemason's hammer. Brick. Edge of the mantelpiece.

He got up and examined the mantel. The corner near the alcove was a possibility, which would mean an accident.

Turning away brusquely, the inspector began to search the room.

He had found nothing of interest by the time he heard voices from the hall below. The voices echoed up to him in a hollow, unnatural way that made him shudder.

He finished his search and went out onto the gallery. Detective Tarkinson was leaving, a short man was coming up the stairs.

Dr. Patcher wore morning dress: homburg, striped trousers, black jacket. He had assumed the outfit when he had been appointed police surgeon. He joked about it himself but didn't like others to.

He was broad, like a shortened wrestler. His cheerful face was dominated by a long nose. He wore spectacles which he continually resettled in place by putting a finger on his nose-tip and sliding it up.

"Greetings," he said, joining Cartland on the gallery. "How's the cough?"

"Better, thanks."

"Heard the latest story on Mrs. Simpson and the king?"

"Ex-king."

"Whatever," the doctor said. "Listen. He used to be the Admiral of the British Fleet, but if he marries her he'll be third mate on an American tramp."

Jack Cartland gave a polite smile. "Talking of tramps," he said. "I thought we'd have one here."

"Interesting case?"

"Could be, Bert. She's a pretty thing."

"You might have yourself a real puzzle."

The inspector gave his fast, massive shrug. "What intrigues me more than puzzles is what the hell she was doing here."

"It'll all come out in the wash," Dr. Patcher said cheerily, hefting his bag. "Let me take a look."

"I'll be downstairs, Bert."

Cartland went down and outside. Constable Pierce and the driver were standing by the police car. To the two men Cartland said:

"Lads, I want you to search the grounds. Be thorough about it. I don't care how long you take."

Pierce asked, "Are we looking for anything in particular, sir?"

"Blunt instrument. That and anything else that looks as if it shouldn't be where you find it. Okay?"

"Yes, sir."

"Get weaving."

The young officers moved off. Inspector Cartland began to pace the gravel thoughtfully. His eyes were on the bulbous toe-caps of his shoes, which surged and ebbed like a pair of playful whales, but what he saw was the study inside.

He tried, Man and woman drive up from London. They break into the house. They're drunk and out for a lark. They go up to that room. They have an argument. He hits her, she dies, he runs.

No problem there. Identify the woman, get the man.

Except, he thought, the build-up couldn't possibly be that straightforward.

Tarkinson appeared. He was carrying his dusting powder in an old soup tin. His brush stuck up from a top pocket. "Smudges," he said. "That window."

"Too bad."

"But I found a smashing one on the bannister," the detective said, like a chairman announcing a loss. "Male right thumb."

"Really? You can tell that much?"

"Absolutely."

Cartland said, grateful and admiring, "You're pretty damn slick at this game."

Footsteps sounded from the hall. "Off you go," the inspector said. "Give that study a thorough check."

"Righto."

Dr. Patcher came out. His homburg was still in place and Cartland wondered inconsequentially if he had worn it all through his examination.

"Pretty girl," he said brightly. "Beautiful teeth."

"Didn't happen to recognise her, I don't suppose."

"No. She may not be local."

The inspector asked, "Was it that blow on the forehead, Bert?"

"Could be—if I don't find a bullet inside her or a pound of arsenic. She looks the thin-cranium type."

"Opinion on the weapon?"

"Anything square," the doctor said, making a right-angle motion with his hand. "A heavy piece of wood could do the trick."

"I'm interested in the time of death."

"About ten last night, I'd say. I'll know more when I get her on the table."

Jack Cartland nodded. He asked, "What about sex? You know, rape or something."

"Nothing apparent. I'll be watching for the signs, of course."

The inspector rubbed the back of his neck. "Well, that's it for now, I think. I'd like you to send me her clothes, jewellery, any papers. Also don't forget to look under her fingernails."

"Leave it to me, Jack," the doctor said, moving toward his car. "Give you a lift, if you're going back."

They got into Patcher's two-seater Morris. As they drove off, Cartland said, "Step number one—identification. Her clothes might do that for us. Labels."

"If she's local, you'd make a short-cut through dentists."

"Yes?"

"Look, her teeth are exceptionally well cared for. She saw a dentist regularly, that girl."

"Good man. Thanks."

When the car drew up outside Stilton's police station, Jack Cartland opened the door and paused. He said, "Bert?"

"Mmm?"

Could she have hit her head on the mantelshelf?

That was the question in his mind. He left it there. He said, "Please let me have her things as quickly as you can."

"Will do, Jack."

Cartland by-passed the main entrance of the police station, a squat and soot-grimed building with all the charm of a heavy frown. He went in by a doorway at the side. Down three steps he was in a stone-floored passage lined with doors and smelling of cheap soap. His office was at the end, a small room with battered equipment and a furtive air.

Waiting there, face anxious, was a young plain-clothes detective, tall and pale, a froth of red hair falling onto his brow. He asked quickly, hovering:

"What's happening, sir? Is it a straight-up murder case? Who's the victim? What've we got so far?"

"Calm down, Keller," the inspector said, holding off a smile. He remembered how he himself had felt when working on his first murder.

Accusingly, Keller said, "You should've telephoned me, sir."

Cartland nodded and sat at his desk. He explained the situation to the detective, who stood by folding and unfolding his arms.

"So that's what we've got so far," the inspector finished. "Sweet nothing."

"What's next?"

"I want you to contact every dentist in town. We've got six. Ring 'em up from the squad room."

"Yes, sir. And say?"

"Ask if they'll be good enough to hold themselves available to go to the hospital mortuary and take a look at a body."

"Right."

Jack Cartland checked his wristwatch. "About an hour from now, when the ambulance had brought her in, I'll call the first and ask him to go along there. If it's no good, I'll call the next one, and so on."

"It's a good idea, sir."

"Well—er—yes."

"What shall I do after that?"

"Get out to Gorse Manor and supervise the search of the grounds."

The red-haired detective was already on his way to the door. "Yes, sir."

Humming, Cartland looked in the telephone directory for the number of the estate agent whom he knew handled the Gorse property. He dialled the firm, spoke to the principal, gave him the news.

When the man had stopped asking questions and saying how terrible, he didn't know what to think, Cartland described the victim and asked if she sounded familiar.

"No. Not at all. Not in the least."

"The keys of Gorse Manor. Are they where anyone can get hold of them?"

"We have two. One is permanently with the caretaker, the other is at present in the possession of Mr. Lunn—Harold Lunn the chartered accountant."

"Is that so?"

"He plans to spend a night in the house next week, looking for ghosts."

"Funny ideas some folk have," the inspector said.

The agent began again on the terribleness and not knowing what to think. Detective Keller looked into the room briefly to raise his thumb: success in alerting the dentists.

Cartland asked the agent about the owners of Gorse Manor, heard nothing of interest, and rang off. He began to make notes for the victim's description, which would be circulated should the dentist approach fail.

Fifteen minutes later, a reporter from the local paper called up. Was it true, he asked, about the two bodies being found in the Gorse place? Jack Cartland set him straight and gave him what facts he wanted to give.

Putting the receiver down, he mused, apropos of the chartered accountant, that a man in the professions would do nicely. Labourer commits murder—no good. Doctor, lawyer, Indian chief—that's news.

And for the second time that morning he felt ashamed of himself, remembering the woman, the young woman, lying dead beside the fireplace.

He went angrily back to his notes.

At nine-thirty Jack Cartland telephoned the first dentist and asked him to go to the morgue. Ten minutes later, Detective Tarkinson came bustling into the office.

He said, "We've got a suspect."

The inspector leaned back heavily in his chair. He had a curious sensation. It was something like alarm.

He stared hard at the man who came in next, followed closely by Constable Pierce. The two were handcuffed together. Pierce was flushed with pleasure. Even Tarkinson looked less glum than usual.

The man was a tramp. Thin, average height, early middle-age, he wore a wreck of an overcoat belted with rope, a woman's long stocking for a scarf, a wellington boot on one foot and on the other a shoe in reasonable condition.

His grey hair and beard formed a single matted mess around his face. He might have been peering through a hole in a shaggy rug. His skin was dirty and pocked with blackheads. Fear showed in his small eyes.

Pierce put a sackcloth bundle on the desk. While the prisoner was being unmanacled and sat in a chair, Jack Cartland opened the bundle. With a distaste which was almost annoyance, he turned over bits of bread, pieces of rag, a medicine bottle half full of milk, two lumps of fatty bacon, a baby's shoe, a small can of beans, five pairs of socks.

Leaning forward, Cartland looked at the man sternly—sternly because it was part of his job. He was thinking, You poor bastard.

The country was full of such men. They were the number one sign of the times. In the early part of the decade they had lost their jobs and had gone, neatly dressed, to look for work in other towns, and then others, and others. As the years passed and jobs stayed elusive, the men sank with their hope.

Their begging became for food, not employment; for a friendly nod, not an open door.

Constable Pierce was telling how he had seen the man, on the Gorse estate, in the trees fifty yards from the house.

"Sort of lurking, sir. You know."

The inspector thought how silly that sounded—lurking. He said, "Yes."

"I shouted at him and he turned and ran. Took off like a shot. I caught up with him easy enough."

"Give you any trouble?"

"No, sir. He came quietly."

"Statement?"

"We asked no questions," Detective Tarkinson said. "Thought we'd leave that up to you."

"Good."

"I did ask him his name. Said it was Smith. No imagination, some people."

Jack Cartland looked at the tramp. He asked, "Where you from, Smith?" He wished he could use *mister*, but it would be bad form at this stage.

The man's gaze was down. His eyes were skipping over a small area of floor, as if even ocular ambition had died.

Hoarsely he said, "Kent."

"Address?"

"Got none."

"Don't be thick. Everyone's got an address."

"Been on the road all me life."

Could be, the inspector thought. Could also be he didn't want anyone from his respectable past to know about his low present. And could be he was on the run from the law.

"Got a police record?"

"No."

Cartland stated, "You telephoned us here at the station last night."

Smith looked up quickly. "Eh?"

Cartland held the frightened stare. He said, "About the dead woman in Gorse Manor."

"No."

"No what?"

"Don't know what you mean."

"You should, Smith," the inspector said. "You killed her, after all."

The man shrank into himself and looked down again. He said, whispering, "Don't know what you're talking about."

Innocent, Jack Cartland thought. Probably.

Relieved, he went on with his questions. He hopped on and around the main theme.

What had Smith been doing at the house? Did he know he'd left his fingerprints on the window he'd broken? Age? Height? When had he last been in jail? What was the woman's name? Where had he spent last night? If he was innocent, why had he tried to run away when challenged by the constable?

Once, between questions to the tramp, he pantomimed one to Constable Pierce: Any resemblance between this man's voice and that of the anonymous caller? Pierce gestured a not-sure.

The telephone rang. It was the dentist. He had seen the dead woman and she was unknown to him. Cartland thanked the man, clicked the cradle, dialled the next of the six dentists and asked him to visit the morgue.

"Yes," the inspector said, looking back at the tramp, "you're our man all right. Care to make a statement?"

Smith shook his head. "No."

"Tell you what. I'm going to put you in a cell to think it over. You'll see that confession's the best for everybody." He nodded at Pierce.

When the constable had left with his prisoner, Detective Tarkinson asked, "Think he's a hot one, sir?"

Jack Cartland gave one of his big, jerky shrugs. "Too early to say."

"Shall I put him on a charge?"

"No. No problem about that. We can hold him for trespassing if we need to. Take the usual precautions, get his prints, give him a cup of hot tea and a sandwich."

"Righto."

Alone, Cartland looked again at the tramp's pathetic collection of possessions. He lifted the baby shoe. It was pink. He dropped it suddenly, feeling he had no right to this familiarity.

Moving to a typewriter stand, he began pecking out a description of the tramp. It would be sent to police headquarters of every county and, accompanied by fingerprints, to Scotland Yard.

The inspector hummed as he worked.

He was still typing when the telephone rang with the call from dentist number two. "I've seen the body," he said. "And she's Mrs. Harold Lunn."

The moonlight picked out gleams on the black car as it drove through quiet streets. Most of those few abroad ignored the car. A long-courting couple watched it go by out of boredom. A beat constable made a point of not showing recognition for the occupant-driver.

The car turned a corner and came into Piper Street. The driver slowed to a stop outside a house midway along. Before he could switch off the engine, the house door opened.

Harold Lunn stepped outside. He looked up and down the street quickly. No one would have heard the car, he thought; he hadn't himself until the last moment; he had been watching for it, the door open a crack.

Assured, he strode to the car and got in beside the driver. He said quietly, "Good evening, Inspector."

"Evening, Mr. Lunn," Jack Cartland said. He set the car in motion.

"Nice night."

"Very pleasant."

"The rain's holding off nicely."

"It is that."

Harold thought they might be friends instead of what amounted to enemies, cat and mouse. The false politeness was absurd. He leaned back in his seat tiredly.

Harold Lunn had aged over the past week. Each day had served him as would a year—a bad one. The rigidity of his tall thin body had eased off, replaced by a slack hesitancy, while his grave manner had increased. He seemed to have shrivelled slightly, like a drying apple on a shelf.

Under his eyes were dark streaks. His mouth had a looseness, was as lax as a sleeper's. Hands which between rest had been wont to make firm gestures and form confident steeples had over the past days taken on furtive habits: clenching, intertwining, massaging.

These changes were due to fear and grief. The fear was for himself, the grief for the loss of the woman he had loved.

Harold felt it welling in him now, the sadness, as it did a score of times every day. It would lift from the steady ache of deadness, start on a pitch like growing hysteria. Sometimes he let it come.

This time he battled. Sitting straighter, he ran a hand over his thinning hair and said, "You know the way, of course."

"Yes."

"Do you still think this is foolish?"

"Mr. Lunn," the inspector said, looking around briefly, "I'm willing to try anything."

"That's a sensible attitude."

"I suppose so. Hope so."

Harold's emotion was settling. He leaned forward and looked at the road ahead. He told himself that in time he would learn to cope. After all, it had been only a week.

When he awoke on the morning of May 17, he found the other bed empty. That was not unusual, for Rosalind was generally the first up. But she never made her bed this early. It had not been slept in.

Harold sat staring at the neat covers, as if he might find there direction, and remembered the events of last night: following Rosalind, entering Gorse Manor, seeing the man in the hall, hearing the two of them up in the study, leaving, the seance at Mrs. Foster's, the return to an empty bedroom.

She could have spent the night on the living-room couch, Harold thought, getting up to dress and wash. He didn't believe it. There was no sound from below. On this level, he could hear faint noises from the boarder's room.

Harold wondered without feeling, not believing this either, where he would find the letter of farewell.

He went downstairs. Rosalind was not there. Nor could he see a letter. Perhaps it would come by post, he thought. Perhaps there would be no notification at all that she had gone away with another man. Perhaps she hadn't.

Harold decided to act as normal for the time being. He left the house after gulping a cup of coffee and leaving a note for the boarder: *Please make own breakfast. Mrs. Lunn gone out.*

He drove to work, went into his own office, and closed the door. With no pretence at working, he sat at his desk and went over every detail of the ugliness which had begun with his reading of Rosalind's diary. He was able to find no innocent, plausible explanation for it all.

He tried to light his pipe, found he was too nervous, and spent five minutes in a frantic search of drawers. The cigarettes he found were stale. He didn't care. The burning of the smoke in his throat was a blessing.

At eleven o'clock there was a tap on the door. "Come in," he called.

His chief clerk entered. He was a small, gnome-like man of sixty with a bald pate and a ruff of white hair. He said:

"A gentleman to see you, sir."

"Yes?"

The clerk glanced at the card in his hand. "Inspector J. Cartland of the Criminal Investigation Department."

Harold experienced a charge of relief. He thought, An accident. She was on her way home to me and got knocked down by a car.

Standing, he said, "Show him in, please."

The policeman was big and middle-aged and sober-faced. Harold vaguely recalled having met him at town council functions.

They shook hands, sat down. Harold reached below sight and clasped his knees. "What can I do for you, Inspector?"

"Mr. Lunn," Cartland said, his face stony, "I'll come straight to the point. It's about your wife."

"Go on, please."

"When was the last time you saw her, sir?"

Harold kept his voice steady. He didn't like this. He didn't like its oddness, didn't like the policeman's gravity.

"Last night, as a matter of fact. She'd gone out when I got up this morning."

"At what time last night?"

"Oh, eight-thirty or so."

"You went out yourself?"

"Yes."

"And she wasn't home when you got back."

"Right. She went to the pictures, I imagine."

The policeman nodded. His gravity had increased. He said, "Mr. Lunn, I'm going to tell you something, a tragic possibility, and then I'd like you to accompany me to the mortuary."

"What?" Harold asked faintly. He felt cold. "Mortuary? What for?"

"For the purposes of identification, Mr. Lunn."

Harold began to get up, staring the while at Inspector Cartland. He had no feelings other than the coldness. His mind was strangely empty. When he had reached his full height he said, "Go on."

"I think your wife is dead, sir."

That was the beginning of a ridiculous hour.

Through it, at times, he was conscious of wearing a small smile, one which lifted up a corner of his mouth. He gave it first when the policeman offered his possibility, which was insane, not tragic; again when, sitting in the back of a police car with Cartland, the older man said:

"I have to tell you, sir, that the lady in question has been murdered."

Ridiculous and ridiculous.

They drove to the County Hospital and around to the back. There was one door marked EMERGENCY, another that called itself MORGUE. They entered the latter, after by-passing a clutch of garbage cans.

A lobby, painted green, smelling of pear-drops. Two nuns were talking with a man at a counter. Another man sat on one of the chairs which sided the room; sat with legs outstretched and eyes closed. He, like the others, was absurd.

Cartland had left. He came back to where Harold was standing by the entrance and said, "We'll have to wait a few minutes."

Harold gave his smile.

He was empty and cold. He smoked mechanically the cigarette handed to him and lit by the inspector. He wondered what there would be for lunch today.

He asked, "Is your wife a good cook?"

The policeman shook his head.

Harold's cigarette was finished and out. He was on the point of asking for another when a door opened, an arm beckoned.

They went into a long, narrow room bright with windows. Under the light were rows of trestle-tables. The smell of pear-drops was stronger.

They stopped beside a table on which rose a low tent of

green cloth. At its end, a towel covered what might have
been the feet of an extra-tall camper.

A man lifted the towel. Revealed was Rosalind's face. She
was asleep.

Cartland asked, "Is this Mrs. Harold Lunn, your wife?"

"Of course," he said. "Of course." Ridiculous.

He would have reached out to wake her but the policeman
took his arm, steered him around, and drew him away.

He was conscious of voices, movements, the sound of a
car: all was confusion. Next, calm had come and he was in a
bleak office, sat facing Inspector Cartland across a desk.

Harold began to laugh. The spasm lasted mere seconds. He
clamped both hands to his mouth, one over the other. He felt
a prickle of tears, an ache in his chest.

The absurdity was over.

Inspector Cartland asked a solicitous, "Are you all right?"

Harold nodded, took a deep breath, lowered his hands.
"Yes."

"If you'd like to go home, Mr. Lunn, you only have to say
so. You've had a great shock."

Harold asked, "She's really dead?"

"Yes."

"Murdered?"

"It looks that way, yes."

"Where did it happen?"

"In Gorse Manor."

"Who did it?"

"We don't know yet."

I know, Harold thought. Her lover did it. He had to be the
one if she died in Gorse Manor. But I don't know who he is
and I can't tell of knowing about him because I'd be
suspected, the cuckold avenger, and I can't tell about being
there last night because I'd be suspected again and I want to
go home to Rosalind.

"Mr. Lunn," the policeman asked, "are you up to answering a few questions? The faster we work, the better."

"I'm all right."

"Fine."

A stenographer was brought, also a cup of hot, sweet tea. Drink finished, the questioning began.

Domestic relations with wife. Her friends. Any romance. Her destination last night. Knowledge of a man named Smith. Valuables or cash in the deceased's possession. Her friends. Her domestic relations with husband.

The repetition became an aggravation. More than once Harold complained, "I've already told you that, Inspector."

"So you did, so you did."

The policeman seemed particularly interested in the unimportant: Michael Shield and the key to Gorse Manor. They were the points he returned to most.

"Do you think," he said, "there could have been anything between Shield and Mrs. Lunn?"

"Not in a million years. He's practically backward."

"They spent a lot of time together, it appears."

"She treated him like a child."

The session was interrupted when a detective with a sad face came in. He had a piece of paper and an ink pad.

The inspector said, "Would you mind, Mr. Lunn, if we took your fingerprints? Just a formality."

"Of course not."

It was a messy business of rolling each fingertip on the pad and then repeating that roll on the paper. Throughout the operation, Harold talked. He couldn't seem to stop himself. He talked about the weather, football, and the engagement of one of his junior clerks.

The detective went, leaving with Harold a piece of cloth soaked in petrol. He worked with close care on his blackened fingers and was grateful for the chore.

"Right," Inspector Cartland said. "Now let me go back and see if I've got these things right. You were at Mrs. Foster's between about nine and eleven."

"Yes."

"You can't be more exact?"

"No," Harold said, sighing with resignation. He felt ill.

"The key then. You've had it for three weeks."

"That's right."

"In your wallet, yes. Your wife knew it was there, I imagine."

"I suppose so."

"And you still have it?"

For the second time, Harold produced the key. He held up the rusty shape. "There."

"If it's all right with you, sir, I think I'd like to have it. After all, I don't suppose you'll be planning on your search for ghosts now."

"No."

The inspector took the key. He tapped it in the palm of his bulbous hand. "The thing is, Mr. Lunn, I'm trying to find a reason for your wife being in the house, and a way she got in there."

"Of course."

"You say you had the key last night and that you did not go with her."

"Correct."

The policeman shook his head. He said, "If you, sir, the lady's husband, can't think of what she was doing there, it's going to be pretty hard for us at the station."

"Something did just occur to me," Harold said. Laying the piece of cloth on the desk, he spoke in a deliberate way, listening to himself. He liked the idea. There was a good chance of it being true. He may have misinterpreted the diary.

"What about this, Inspector," he said. "Rosalind, who has always scoffed at my interest in the supernatural, decides to play a trick on me. She went to Gorse Manor last night simply to make arrangements, fix up some sort of imitation ghost that she could show on the twenty-third."

"How did she get in?"

"That I don't know. It might come out. But what d'you think of the idea?"

Inspector Cartland nodded slowly. "It's not bad," he said. "Not bad at all. It could explain her presence, it doesn't explain her death."

"She surprises a burglar?"

"Nothing in there to attract a thief, Mr. Lunn."

Harold went on thinking about his theory. It helped keep the fact of death away.

He noticed that Inspector Cartland was looking past him, toward the doorway. He turned. As he did so, a man who was standing there swung around and left. It was the glum detective.

Harold looked back at Inspector Cartland, who asked, glancing down at his notes:

"You say you were not in Gorse Manor last night?"

"Yes."

The policeman looked up. "Mr. Lunn, your fingerprint was found on the bannister."

Harold blinked. Now he had a totally new emotion. He said, "It sounds as though I'm on your list of suspects."

"All I'm doing, sir, is stating a fact. Your print is there."

"A week or so ago," Harold said, "just after I got the key, I went in the house to scout about. My fingerprints could be all over the place."

"Was anyone with you that day?"

"No."

"Did you tell anyone you were going?"

"My wife."

"Anyone else?"

Harold made a shrug. It was not as casual as it looked. "Not that I can recall."

"I see," Inspector Cartland said. "So we only have your word for it that you were in the house previous to last night."

"Well, I suppose so."

The policeman looked down again at his notes. From his

expression and manner it was impossible for Harold to tell how seriously he was taking this line of conjecture.

Cartland said, "You mentioned, I believe, that you had no children."

Harold sighed. "Look, Inspector. I'm tired. If it's all the same to you, I'd like to go home."

Cartland looked up quickly. "Any time you want, Mr. Lunn. You only have to say."

"I'm saying. I want to go home."

"Right."

They got up and walked to the office door, where Cartland said, "If you should plan on leaving town, I'd appreciate it if you'd let me know where I can get hold of you."

"Very well. But I'm not going anywhere, Inspector."

"And would you please ask Mr. Shield to hold himself available for questioning?"

"Yes, I'll do that."

The policeman put out his hand. "Mr. Lunn, please accept my condolences on your loss."

Harold felt a rise of emotion. Shaking hands quickly, he strode out.

On the street, the moment he passed outside, Harold was shocked immobile and thoughtless by a flash of light. It exploded in his face like a flare.

After it, he saw two men approaching. One had a large camera.

The other man, notebook in hand, asked, "Mr. Harold Lunn?"

"What?"

"We're reporters and we'd like—"

Harold brushed past and walked on swiftly. He began to understand that Rosalind's death was a beginning as well as an end. There would be endless formalities and crudities and complications. Reporters. Letters from and to friends. Funeral arrangements. Legalities. The service and burial. The inquest. The trial.

Who would be tried?

Harold assured himself firmly that he was not a prime suspect. He would, naturally, be on the list. But the police were not fools. They would soon dig up the lover's identity.

Crossing the High Street, Harold went into a shop's recessed doorway. He looked back along the street. Thankfully he saw no signs of the two reporters.

About to move on, he noticed that the shop was a tobacconist's. He went in and bought four packets of Players. Opening one as he came out, he hurriedly lit a cigarette. He drew viciously deep at the smoke.

Farther along the street he turned into his firm's doorway. The head clerk rose from his desk in the hall. To him Harold said, without preamble:

"Mrs. Lunn died last night. Carry on here, will you, please?"

Leaving the gnome-like man gaping, he went on down the hall, out through the rear of the building and along an alley to his car. He drove off.

The direction he was taking, he saw, was that of Gorse Manor. He didn't know why. He lit a fresh cigarette from the stub of the old.

Nearing the Gorse gatehouse, Harold saw there a group of people, ten or fifteen strong. They were simply standing and staring up the driveway.

It's true, Harold thought.

He made a U-turn and headed for home. On the way, all he thought about was how strangely normal everything looked. People were talking, business was going on, the sun shone. Strange.

He was particularly disturbed to see a man and woman laughing. He turned to look back at the couple when he had driven by.

In Piper Street, Harold was relieved to see no repetition of the scene at the gatehouse. He parked carefully and went into the house.

Michael Shield was in the living room, reading by the fire. As blank of face as always, he lay down his book and said:

"You're home early, Mr. Lunn."

Glancing at his watch, Harold saw that the time was two o'clock. He had been with the police for three hours.

Shield said, "Mrs. Lunn isn't back yet. I made my own lunch."

Harold walked to the window. He looked out at the small, neat garden. It seemed foolish and pointless.

He said, "My wife isn't coming back." He blinked with astonishment.

"What?"

"My wife is never coming back. She was killed last night."

Harold turned. The reason he didn't look at Michael Shield was that he had almost forgotten his existence. He had remembered Mrs. Foster.

Looking at the telephone, he thought, Too risky.

He hurried out of the house.

———————◄◆►———————

The police car turned into a lane on the outskirts of town. On one side were cottages, on the other tall trees. Before the car's headlights swung into position, the moonlight hung black shrouds of shadow between the branches and the roadway.

There was no one about. Some of the cottages were already dark in sleep. All that was heard was the motor and the tyres scuffling the dried mud.

"It's nice out here," Inspector Cartland said.

"Yes."

"Always fancied a bit of the country life."

Harold Lunn said, "It's that one there."

"Yes, I know."

The inspector brought the car to a stop by a white-painted gate. Thirty feet back from the neat dry-stone wall into which the gate was set, the cottage stood prettily. It was whitewashed, attended by flowers and roofed in heavy slate.

Switching off the engine, Inspector Cartland eased his bulk out and went to the rear of the car. He unlocked the luggage compartment. Its lid he lifted quietly, not wishing to disturb the silence.

Harold Lunn had also alighted. He pushed back the gate and walked to the cottage. His knock was gentle.

Mrs. Foster opened the door. "Good evening," she said. "I'm all ready."

She had a coat on and a muffler pinned across her throat. The scarf tied around her head was new, as though this were an occasion worthy of that some special thing.

While Harold Lunn murmured a greeting, Mrs. Foster tried not to look at his face. The wretchedness there made her unhappy.

"Shall I take the box?" he asked.

"Yes, please."

Harold Lunn stepped inside. From where it leaned against the wall by the door, he picked up a slender crate. It was three feet square and two inches deep.

"That's everything?" he said.

"Yes. We can go."

They went out. Mrs. Foster locked up carefully. Harold Lunn took the box to the car and put it in the luggage compartment.

Inspector Cartland was standing by the open back door. He said gravely, "Good evening, ma'am."

"Evening, Mr. Cartland."

"Mild tonight."

"Very pleasant," Mrs. Foster said. She got into the back.

The two men got in the front and the car moved off. Harold Lunn glanced behind to ask, "Do you mind if I smoke, Mrs. Foster?"

"Not at all. Please do."

But she didn't like it. Not the smoke in the car, that was no trouble, she wasn't bothered by the smell of cigarettes. What she didn't like was her friend's constant need to settle his nerves. He had been through a heartbreaking ordeal, and it was still going on.

Yet tonight might see an end to it, Mrs. Foster thought.

She sat forward tensely as her mind went to what lay ahead. In equal parts, she was frightened and thrilled.

And all because of what happened on the sixteenth, she mused.

———◆—◆———

She drew her door open, saying, "You're late, Mr. Lunn. I'd just about given you up."

"Late? I hadn't noticed."

"Not that it matters. There's only you and me this evening."

"Fine."

"How about a nice cup of coffee?"

"Yes," he said. "It is a nice evening."

She gave him a quick glance. He looked preoccupied.

Not himself tonight, she thought. It's that business of his and all those problems. Too much brain work. Worry worry worry. He could do with a break away from everything. Sea air. Skegness. Southport.

"What a shame you're not going away for a holiday this year, Mr. Lunn."

"Yes," he said absently. He was standing in the middle of the room, gazing at the fire.

"Still, I expect as you'll be able to snatch a weekend or two."

"Mm?" he said, looking around. "Oh yes. Quite so."

Uncomfortable and sympathetic, Mrs. Foster gestured toward the table on which lay her Ouija board. "We might as well start."

The seance was not a success. Mr. Lunn had never been so

distracted. Twice he even took his finger off the cup. Few were the coherent words the board spelled out, and they appeared to be meaningless.

After her visitor had gone, Mrs. Foster made cocoa and sat by the fire. She was depressed. Not only about Mr. Lunn—that was a passing thing—but about all connected with the occult. Year after year, she seemed to be getting no closer.

Mrs. Foster had always deliberately played down her gift. Not merely to other people, also to herself. She was not sure that she liked her peculiar ability. She had the feeling that there were some things you shouldn't meddle with. And it didn't seem right somehow that she, an uneducated woman, should have been given this strange talent—if that's what it was.

When she had first tried on a makeshift board, at a friend's house, using bits of paper marked with letters, she had felt suddenly quite different. There had been a throb in her arm, for one thing. The throb, which had a slight ache, extended from behind the shoulder to the wrist. Also there was an odd sensation in her head, a dreaminess, like when she was trying to wake up fully from her afternoon nap.

The upturned glass had spelled the Christian name of her dead father. Someone accused her, joshingly, of cheating by pushing the glass. Alarmed by the appearance of the name, she had lied, "Yes, I did."

She had taken up the practice in earnest, despite being fearful. She was unable to resist. There was no response when she sat alone, but the throb and dreaminess nearly always came when others were present. Results were sometimes pointless, sometimes disturbingly relevant.

However, she had continued to insist on the modesty of her gift, and had refused to take money from her sitters. She was unable to make up her mind whether what she was doing was good or evil.

When she met Harold Lunn, he swayed her toward the

former. She began to harbour fancies of absolute success with this man who knew so much about the supernatural.

There had been progress with Mr. Lunn, yes. But not enough. What she wanted to know now was: Did she possess a rare quality, or was she just a silly old woman? Was it, in fact, worth going on?

Mrs. Foster sighed, finished her cocoa, and went to bed.

The next day, after lunch, she was called outside by her neighbour, a woman her own age. The neighbour was leaning over the fence, face flushed and eager.

"It's a murder," she said breathlessly. "They found this murdered woman in Gorse Manor. She was done in last night."

"Good heavens."

"Yes but listen, listen. This is the thing. You'll never guess. She's the wife of Harry Lunn's boy. *Your* Mr. Lunn. I met him myself at your house. Twice. Think of it."

Anxiously she added, "You haven't heard already, have you?"

Mrs. Foster was stunned. She said, "I don't believe it. Mrs. Lunn? Never."

The neighbour added vigorously, "True as true. On my mother's grave. I got it on the telephone from our Mary, and she got it from young Peg, you know, what works for the dentist. He said . . ."

The woman talked on, piling up details like dirty dishes. Mrs. Foster believed. It had to be true.

She got away from the neighbour as soon as she politely could. Inside, she sat close to the fire. Although she had never met Mrs. Lunn, she felt sad over her death, sickened that it was murder. In connexion with Mr. Lunn, she kept to a feeling of pity, avoiding the cogitation that would lead to the way he had acted last night.

Mrs. Foster was still sitting in her chair when she heard a car stop on the lane. Getting up, she saw through the window who the caller was. She went to open the door.

Mr. Lunn came in. His hands were deeply pocketed, his head was down. He was pale and grim. He gave no greeting. Pacing the small room, he said:

"I followed my wife last night when she went out. She went to Gorse Manor. I think she planned a trick for me next week. I followed her inside and then I left. Soon after that, she was murdered. It's possible the police suspect me."

He stopped walking, looked at Mrs. Foster where she stood by her chair. "Sorry," he said. "I should have started with the news of Rosalind's death."

"I heard already."

"Yes?"

"A neighbour told me."

"It's probably all over town by now."

"I'm terribly sorry, Mr. Lunn." It seemed inadequate, but she could think of nothing else to say. In any case, it occurred to her that he looked more like a fugitive than a mourner.

"Thank you," he said.

"Can I get you something? I've got sherry."

"I actually came to ask for your help. I haven't told anyone else about being at Gorse Manor last night. No one knows but us, you and I. I told you the truth because I trust you."

"Thank you, Mr. Lunn."

He looked away and started pacing again. "I'm going to ask you to lie for me. If necessary to lie under oath. I want you to say that I came here about nine last night. It was closer to ten, I think."

"Quarter to."

"Say you don't remember exactly but it was about nine. That makes it sound better."

Mrs. Foster nodded, asking, "Are the police going to come here?"

"Sure to," he said. "And the problem is, they found my fingerprints in the house."

"Oh."

"Obviously I left them there when I looked the place over.

I probably mentioned to you that I was going to do that."

"I can't remember."

Changing course, he came to stand in front of her. A good measure of his agitation seeped out of him. He unpocketed one hand and held it out, palm up.

"Mrs. Foster," he said evenly. "I didn't kill my wife."

She nodded, widening her eyes with sincerity. "I believe you."

"As God is my judge, I'm innocent."

"I believe you. I really do."

"I don't know who did kill her. I suspected a lover. That's the reason I was a bit on edge last night."

"I understand, Mr. Lunn."

"You'll help me?".he asked. His manner was more tiredly resigned than imploring. "You'll lie to the police?"

"Of course."

"Bless you," he said. He turned away quickly and left the house. Through the window she saw him hurry to the car and drive off.

With furious energy, Mrs. Foster set about washing the kitchen floor, which she had scrubbed two days before. In the moments when the work failed to intrude, she blinked away tears for her sadness or gasped her shock or smiled at being able to help or tightened her lips to counter the dread of a police interrogation.

She was brushing the hall carpet when she heard her neighbour call out. Knowing her visitor must have been seen, and that she was expected to add inside details to the story, she answered that she was busy.

It was late afternoon when they came. Dropping the chamois with which she had been cleaning the back windows, Mrs. Foster went with forced calm to the front door.

She was met by the unexpected. Instead of several grim policemen whose uniform buttons glinted like knives, there was one middle-aged man in untidy clothes, clumsy-handed and with a lumpy face.

When she had brought the visitor inside, Mrs. Foster surprised herself by asking him if he would like a cup of tea.

"Lovely," he said, sitting back comfortably in the chair she had proffered. "I've been on the go all day."

She fetched him a sandwich as well, lettuce and tomato. There was no interrogation. They had a chat. The policeman, who gave his name as Jack Cartland, talked about the murder and how upsetting it was for everybody, and how they had a man called Smith who might have done it.

"That's good," Mrs. Foster said. "I'm glad you've caught someone."

"Yes, but I'm worried about that Mr. Lunn. He seems a decent bloke."

"Oh he is. A fine man."

Jack Cartland swallowed the last of his sandwich. "The only way we can help him is if we get the absolute truth about his movements. He's a bit fuzzy himself. I'd be the same after a shock like that."

"He's terribly upset, poor man. He looks ill."

"Yes," Jack Cartland said. He glanced down to brush crumbs off his lap. "I can understand him coming to see you this afternoon, you two being such friends."

"That's what friends are for, after all."

They talked about the times of Mr. Lunn's arrival and departure the night before, of his fingerprints, of his home life.

"Get on, did they?" Jack Cartland asked.

"Very well, I should think. Leastways, he never said any other."

"I wonder if he ever mentioned his girl friend to you. You might even know her, come to think of it."

Mrs. Foster blinked. "A girl friend? Oh no. That doesn't sound like Mr. Lunn. Are you sure?"

The policeman scratched his bristly hair. "I'm not, to be honest. It was something I heard. Could be gossip."

"I'm sure it is," she said firmly.

"He's not the type to have lady friends?"

"Definitely not."

Until Jack Cartland left, they chatted about Gorse Manor. As he was walking down the path, a constable on a motorcycle roared up and came to a stop by the car. Mrs. Foster stayed in her doorway. Jack Cartland and the constable talked together. Their attitude was urgent.

Mrs. Foster felt compelled to walk toward her gate. She reached it as the constable turned away and got back on his machine. He roared off.

Face thoughtful, Jack Cartland came slowly to the gate. He said, "Well, Mrs. Foster, there's a grim bit of news if you like."

"What is it?"

His shoulders made a large, fast shrug. "He's killed himself."

Mrs. Foster gasped. Both hands leapt to her chest and clutched one another tightly. Her arms were quiveringly stiff. It was as though each hand was trying to throw the other off, claim possession.

She whispered, "What?"

"Suicide."

"Oh my good God."

"In his cell," Jack Cartland said. "They just found him."

"What?"

"That tramp. Smith."

Mrs. Foster sagged forward onto the gate.

———◆▶———

The street-lamps were brighter and more numerous here, killing the moonlight. People strolled. The business places which had begun to spot the long, suburban street were growing larger and more frequent. The marquee of a cinema blazed light and pictures of Mae West.

The police car moved steadily, heading for the centre of

town. Since leaving the cottage, the three occupants had been silent.

Mrs. Foster sat tensely in the back and, to maintain calm, pretended she was simply out for a drive. Harold Lunn smoked quickly and nervously, his lungs hardly emptied of smoke before he was again drawing on the cigarette. Through the partially open window beside him, a blue haze of smoke was moving in a constant, wavering stream.

Inspector Cartland had the most self-possession, though he was by no means his normal tranquil self. The fat fingers of one hand were drumming on the wheel. Occasionally he would start to hum, and then, realising the act, would break it off abruptly.

Now, beginning to find the silence a strain, the inspector cut it with a question to which he already knew the answer:

"Which hotel is it?"

"The Grand," Harold Lunn said.

"Nice place."

"So I believe."

The inspector shuffled in his seat. "You know, if there's one part of tonight I really don't go along with, it's this."

"I think it's a good idea. So does Mrs. Foster."

"Yes," the medium said. "I do. A very good idea."

The silence gone, everyone seemed eager to keep it away.

"I just don't see that it's necessary," Inspector Cartland went on. "The three of us should be enough."

"He and my wife were close."

Mrs. Foster: "It can't do any harm. It might do a lot of good."

"Very close," Harold Lunn said. "Perhaps he brought out the mother instinct in her." That surprised him. What he added was another surprise. "Perhaps she saw him as the child she never had."

"There you are," Mrs. Foster said.

The inspector nodded. "That's possible. Yes, I can see that."

He brought the car to a halt at a red traffic signal. The light somehow acted also as a stop on the talk. All three tried to think of something else to say. Failing, giving up, they turned their minds to the subject of the brief conversation: Michael Shield.

———◆———

After the death of his parents, Michael went to live with Aunt Maude. Her house was neat and fussily pretty, like a starched ruff with lace on the edges. The thrice-weekly cleaning woman did only the heavy work, had strict orders to keep away from the ornaments and trimmings. In the front room, where the house's character reached its doll apex, the very idea of moving inside from the doorway was disturbing; only an insensitive boor could have sat there in ease.

Apart from the exchange of homes, Michael's life was outwardly little different from before. He stayed on at his old job, declining the offer of a transfer to the railway station near his new home. The mere thought of beginning all over again with unknown people made him sweat. He bought a bicycle for the journey between suburbs.

His father's will probated, Michael found himself in a smug position financially. Although he was unable to touch the capital, the income it paid him was equal to that of three average workers. He accepted the situation with indifference. Money had never been one of his interests.

The routine of his days was firmly fixed. He arose at seven, made breakfast for himself, and cycled to work, arriving at eight. His morning consisted of handling suitcases and parcels, giving out tickets for these and accepting the charges. Lunch he took in the station's refreshment room, where the girls treated him with friendly familiarity and sometimes made crude remarks to see him blush. The afternoon was a repeat of the morning. At five o'clock he began the journey back. Evenings were spent reading, listening to the wireless, or playing dominoes with Aunt Maude. Once a week they went to the cinema together.

On Friday evenings, Michael gave Aunt Maude two-thirds of his wage packet, to pay for his keep. She always said the same thing: "Oh well. If you insist." Saturday afternoons Michael walked around the town centre. Like a pensioner for whom time ached, he dawdled through Woolworths and Littlewoods and the British Home Stores. He bought small items for which he had no use and which he sometimes threw away before reaching home. In the Kardomah Cafe he lingered over a cup of coffee and a bun, while partaking of the conversations around him. He climaxed the outing with a browse in the W. H. Smith bookshop. He always bought at least three books.

Sunday mornings, Michael and Aunt Maude went to church, a medium-scale Anglican. Michael was a communicant out of politeness. He had no faith; or, more to the core, he never paused to consider if he had. Religion for him was part of the social scheme, like covering your mouth when yawning. The services he sat through mindlessly, except for the concern of keeping his eyes averted from crucifixes, which repelled him.

After the traditional heavy Sunday lunch of the English, ever devoted to the pursuit of discomfort, Michael went to his room for a nap. That was followed by a walk. Next came high tea, another assault on the system. Sometimes there would be guests at the meal, cousins or neighbours. Afterwards, reading or dominoes, and an early night in view of the 7 A.M. rising.

A dull enough life. But placid. Or so it might appear. Michael was far from serene inside.

Anxiety was his constant companion, his treacherous friend, his cross without the bleeding Jesus. Every day and in every place, nameless dreads hovered around him like pigeons. He didn't know why he worried so, or what it was that gave him worry.

If, as happened on occasion, he concluded that this was not a normal state of affairs, that other people were not similarly harassed, he offered himself the explanation he had once overheard from his aunt and his stepmother: He was odd; very odd.

There were no pressures at work—other than those his anxiety invented. His superior in the left-luggage office was a tyrant only in respect of his own cleanliness, a man who cared more about the state of his fingernails than the labours of those under his command. Michael's work mates had long since given up jeering at him for what to them were his frailties; if they acknowledged his presence at all, it was with casual camaraderie.

At home there were no tribulations. Advancing years and companionship had rent broad fissures in Aunt Maude's hard shell. Her manner and voice were milder, her smile was more in evidence. She had begun to mellow. Now she was tolerant of Michael's clumsiness and his forgetting of rules, which, in any case, had been allowed to soften.

Aunt Maude treated her nephew almost as an equal. She often told him how big he was getting to be.

Michael suffered. He brooded and fretted and never left his worry behind. The pigeons were always there, besmirching the statue they adored.

And the times between Michael's bouts of insulting females grew shorter.

After degrading that woman in the park on the day of his parents' funeral, six months had passed before he performed a similar act. The next time was four months later; then three. The period settled to an average of six weeks.

Each venture started in the same way. Michael would experience low down in his stomach a tingling sensation. With breaks during bouts of mental activity, it continued for several days, growing stronger like the pain of a rotting tooth. Michael's anxiety increased. That he had at least the satisfaction of owning a name for his dread was cancelled by the dread itself.

He always told himself that this time he would fight. And he would win. He was definitely not going to do that corrupt thing. Never again. It was terrible and shameful. It was also criminal.

Fight he did, yet he always lost. The tingling became unbearable, an itch beyond reach of the physical scratch. It was like a boil that yearned for the lance. He tried violent activity, meditation, visits to church. Nothing worked to save him. He had to find easement. He had to answer that strange call.

Finally he would set out. One part of him was still fighting, the other was craftily making plans.

He cycled to one of several nearby parks and recreation areas. Never did he visit the same one twice in a row. Leaving his bicycle, he walked.

His recipient he chose with care, and didn't mind spending an hour or more on the task. The woman had to be alone, settled in one place, and well separated from other people. Most important, she had to be older than Michael.

There were other factors to be taken into consideration. A nearby dog might belong to the woman and be a potential danger. The light had to be good. There must be nobody who might approach over the following minutes or come within earshot.

So many elements were there, in fact, that the still-fighting part of Michael took hope as he walked. But somehow the other part never failed to find the ideal situation.

Emotionally, however, Michael was not always successful —although he didn't think in terms of success or failure. He only knew that sometimes he later felt dull and dissatisfied.

The reaction of the woman fell into three distinct patterns: A, she refused to look at him again after the first glance, keeping her head firmly down or turned away. B, she got up and quickly left. C, she reviled him.

The last was the most frequent. It was not often that Michael had that feeling of dullness and dissatisfaction.

Only once did a woman react outside the three patterns. She smiled at Michael, sat straighter, and said he was standing too far away, he should come closer. He strode off.

Afterwards, in the days following his ventures, came remorse. Michael would fret and fume and despair—while in the background was the lesser concern that the police may be actively working on the case.

How could he bring himself to do this terrible thing? he would rage. Apart from the dirtiness, it was immoral to frighten and shock these inoffensive women, women who had never done him any harm. Why, why, *why* did he do it? And was he going to move on to even more terrible acts? Would he finish up attacking little girls?

Michael was deeply disturbed. He got no relief in trying to put the blame on his alter ego, Little Ben. Furthermore, in addition to being stricken that he had hurt the women, he was also irked, a feeling like envy, which further puzzled and tormented him.

At night in bed he would cry, his head under the covers so Aunt Maude couldn't hear. He swore he would never do the filthy act again. He always believed that, and he always abrogated the oath when, a few weeks later, that familiar, frightening tingle began.

The years passed. Michael reached his majority. Tall, slouched, flabbily plump and with a round baby face, clumsily dressed, he made far from a prepossessing figure. He was shy, awkward, and chewed his fingernails. At gatherings, he instinctively moved to the sidelines.

He didn't smoke. He had never had a date; the three times he corralled sufficient courage to ask a girl out, he received affectionate but solid refusals. He rarely had a drink; on his twenty-first birthday he was taken to a pub by his work mates to celebrate and fell asleep after the second beer.

One evening, arriving home from work, Michael found

Aunt Maude sitting on the kitchen floor. Her face was grey and slack. With a smile of apology she said, "I can't get up. How silly I am." Michael ran for the doctor.

Aunt Maude was taken to hospital. The next day she had an operation, which, a cheerful surgeon told Michael afterwards, was a complete success and the old girl would be up and about in no time. But she stayed on in her hospital bed, growing older and weaker.

Michael was solicitous. He had a continual pain of worry. He visited his aunt every day without a miss throughout the months of her illness. Not once in that time did he get the urge to verbally abuse a woman.

Michael knew Aunt Maude was dying when, one Sunday, he saw that they had shaved off her moustache. She looked dead already. He was profoundly moved. He went home and wept.

It was an anti-climax, the telephone call to his place of work to say that Miss Shield had passed away. Dry-eyed but feeling lost, Michael went home in a taxi. He was off work a week, during which the house was full of people endlessly coming and going. It was the aftermath of his parents' death all over again. Michael coped.

As the months passed, he recovered from his loss, though he became even quieter and more withdrawn than before. He started dozens of plans on what to do with his life, and left each one unfinished.

The estate had been willed equally between himself and a cousin. Michael sold his share of the house to his fellow beneficiary on the understanding that he be allowed to remain there as a tenant. He stayed in the same job. He had, at least, the comfort of the known.

His day-to-day routine was almost the same as before. He read more, went out sometimes to eat, indulged in his daydream with greater frequency; and he shrank to a month the period between acts of emotional outburst.

Apart from those times, there was only one event of prominence until the end came.

One afternoon, cycling home, Michael saw some youths
tormenting a puppy. He jumped off his bicycle and ran to
remonstrate. The boys attacked him. He retaliated, his arms
swinging wildly, his mouth agape in a grimace of anger and
fear.

The skirmish was short. After it, Michael found himself
alone with the puppy in his arms. Shock receding, he felt
nauseated. It was due both to his own physical hurts and the
memory of blood on some of the boys' faces. He vomited
twice on the way home.

He kept the dog. At first he enjoyed its company and its
greeting when he entered the house. Soon, however, he
became uncomfortable with the pup's affection and depend-
ence. He was relieved as well as sad when the dog got run
over on the busy road which he had started to use as an exer-
cise area.

A week later he was in a park, strolling. Twilight had
started, the park had a reassuring paucity of people. Only ten
minutes passed before he saw what he wanted: what he
always thought of previously as a prospect, later as a victim.

The woman was in her early forties, alone and sitting on
the grass on a piece of newspaper, the headline of which
Michael could read. He had the usual clarity of perception of
these outings. He also had a foreboding of disaster—yet this,
too, was fairly normal.

Michael stopped. The tingling sensation was powerful and
making him tremble.

The woman had her eyes on a squirrel. She looked around
when Michael gave a cough, but at once gave her attention
back to the small animal.

Michael coughed twice more and then called out. He said,
"Look."

The woman looked. Michael carefully pronounced a string
of obscene words. The woman stared, her face twisted up in

disbelief. What happened next was outside the pattern, and terrifying.

She screamed.

The sound was like a shrill whistle. Michael turned swiftly away. He ran straight into the arms of a man. A powerful man who held him tightly.

———◆———

The Grand Hotel, on Stilton's High Street, was a tall building of graceful proportions which few people ever noticed because of the street's narrowness there and the lower level of brassy stores.

On that level, the hotel was represented solely by a broad doorway inside which were steps of marble and red carpet. A copper marquee thrusted out elegantly. The place needed only an admiral-like doorman to round out the impression.

The entrance was deserted.

"You'd think he would have been waiting," Mrs. Foster said in mild rebuke. She was impatient.

Inspector Cartland brought the car to a stop in the kerb. He said, "Be chilly, I suppose, standing about."

Mrs. Foster peered up the steps. "Still."

Harold Lunn asked, "Shall I go?"

The inspector shrugged. "It doesn't matter."

The other man opened his door and got out. He went to the yielding red carpet. A lobby opened out, all pillars and palms and hush. Of the handful of non-staff present, one was Michael Shield. He sat in an easy chair, head back, gaze on the ceiling.

Harold Lunn went across. He wondered if this had been such a good idea after all.

"Evening," he said. "Are you ready?"

Michael Shield got up quickly, flurried. He blushed. "Yes. Sorry. Yes, I'm ready. I wasn't sure what time you'd be here."

"Come along."

They went outside and got in the car, Michael in the back. He said again, "I wasn't sure what time you'd be here."

Mrs. Foster, unhappy about her earlier attitude, told the young man, "It doesn't matter."

"Thank you."

"I'm Mrs. Foster, by the way."

"Oh yes. Of course. Michael Shield. How do you do."

"Nice to meet you," she said. She thought what a polite boy, and how innocent-looking. Decent. You could see he needed taking care of.

Inspector Cartland set the car in motion. The exchange in the back had sounded odd. It had not occurred to him that the medium and the boarder had never met. To him, everyone in the case was so familiar, as if he had known them for years, that it hadn't crossed his mind some could be strangers to each other.

Funny, he thought. Bloody funny the whole thing. For anyone with a mad sense of humour.

"Be there in ten minutes," he said, and, forgetting, began to hum.

———————◆———————

There was a morning mist, waist-high, a flimsy white. It lay over the open stretches of ground like crumpled tissues on a dark counterpane. Among the trees, which kept it to a constancy, the mist might have been claiming to be the ghost of the snows of yesterday.

Through the wooded parts moved six men. The smokiness drifted away from their feet as they walked, enabling them to see the ground. This was the second Gorse property search of the investigation.

The darkness of their clothing heightened by the white, the men moved slowly among the trees, their heads down. From where Inspector Jack Cartland stood in the open, they appeared to be looking for their legs.

That's about all they would find, he thought. If Harold Lunn was the man, it was hardly likely he would have thrown the weapon away in leaving.

And the weapon might be the mantelshelf.

That unwelcome thought Cartland turned from by making a turn with his body. He strode off over the weed-captured lawn.

In any case, he reminded himself, it was time he was getting back. He had an appointment with the chief constable.

Jack Cartland yawned. He was tired, though not unpleasantly so. When finally abed last night, he had been kept long awake by nervous hope, an importunate mistress. Before that, he had been busy until late.

There had been the problem of Smith's suicide, reports to type, the meagre evidence to sift and discuss with his team, the autopsy to read, an interview with journalists (three from national papers), and the taking of two crank telephone calls: the mayor was the killer, it was the work of German spies.

There had been the minor chore of going to different shops to buy copies of Stilton's *Evening News*. The murder was the headline story, of course. The paper had gone to press too late to include the suicide. There was a photograph of the inspector and one of Constable Pierce, who had found the body, pictures of Gorse Manor, and one of a startled-looking Harold Lunn. The inspector had bought five copies.

He stepped onto the gravel, passed the manor, and headed along the drive. Earlier he had talked to Mrs. Trent, the caretaker, a stocky and sinister-faced woman who answered his questions caustically. She knew nothing.

Passing the gatehouse, he set out along the road. Soon, houses began. When they firmed to a shoulder-by-shoulder design, he saw the police car. He also saw two detectives talking at the doors of nearby houses.

Cartland waited by the car. Presently, Detective Keller approached. The red-haired man looked pleased with himself.

"That place there, sir," he said, pointing. "A woman. She saw a car on the night in question."

"What time?"

"That's the weakest bit. It could've been any time between eight-thirty and nine-thirty. Says she never bothers about time."

"Lovely."

Keller said, "She can't tell us much about the car either. But it may help."

"Go on."

"She heard car brakes and looked through her curtains. A man got out of a car and walked on. He was going toward Gorse Manor. The car she remembers nothing about. The man, well, he was just tallish."

"Later?"

"Nothing. She had the radio on."

Jack Cartland said, "Have another go at her. Try and jog her memory. When you've made all your calls, take her in and get a statement."

"It's not bad, eh?"

"Who knows, son."

A minute later, however, walking on, Inspector Cartland thought the news interesting and possibly significant. He imagined the scene; Lunn arranges to meet wife at Gorse Manor. Gives her the key. Parks well away from the house. Goes upstairs with wife and kills her. Leaves and goes to Mrs. Foster's.

And how nice it had been of the medium to give out free of charge that Lunn had been to see her yesterday. Curious thing for him to do. Was the visit for sympathy, or to firm the alibi?

Mrs. Foster had sounded genuine enough and open, Cartland mused. But she might sing a different tune if he danced in another style—apache instead of courteous waltz.

Jack Cartland pulled a face at himself, remembering the

kindly widow. He consoled: A copper has to be a bit of a bastard to succeed.

Coming to a bus-stop, he paused and looked back. Should he wait? No. He would stick to his original decision and walk to town. He always thought best when out walking.

Going on, he wondered about the tramp. Why was he so determinedly refusing to accept Smith's suicide as evidence of guilt, or its possibility? But there was nothing to wonder about. He knew why. It was the same reason he was delaying ridiculously long in interviewing the lodger, Michael Shield. He didn't want anyone to be the villain except the husband, a newsmaker because of his professional status and respectability.

So was it merely the publicity, or did he have a real feeling about Lunn's guilt?

A feeling, no. He didn't believe in intuitions. They were for private eyes in fiction. What he believed in was evidence.

Which, he realised, did not properly answer the question.

He walked on firmly.

Fifteen minutes later he entered the police station by its main door. There was a large, bleak, brown-painted room that smelled like a doss-house, victim of a thousand sweaty arguments, a thousand retching drunks.

Behind the counter leaned a sergeant. He was fifty and bald and cheery-sardonic of face. He said:

"Morning, Jack. Papers are in."

"Hello, Sam," Cartland said. "What's new on Smith?"

While listening to the sergeant tell of the "person unknown" responses coming in from around the country, the inspector looked as if with casual interest at the national newspapers lying on the counter.

The case was on every front page, though in the bottom half. Without exception, it was called "The Haunted House Murder." His name was in two of the reports, misspelled in one and prefaced in the other by "Superintendent." Nevertheless, Jack Cartland was thrilled by seeing there what several million others would see.

He looked up. "Where's the press boys now, Sam?"

"I think they're trying to corner Mr. Lunn."

There was an obvious comeback to that. Cartland resisted. He asked, "Anything been happening here?"

"Phone calls," the sergeant said, smiling and shaking his head. "Fifteen at least. Most of 'em wanted to know if it was safe to let their kids go to school. One nut said he wanted protection. Two said they'd seen men lurking near their houses—I sent a man to check on those."

"In other words, a load of bloody nonsense."

"There you go."

"Still," Cartland said, "you never know. Hear them all out."

"Right."

The inspector went on, passed through a doorway, and slowly climbed a flight of stairs. The wooden steps boomed beneath him like deep-lung coughing.

The door said CHIEF CONSTABLE OF STILTON. Cartland tapped and entered. The room had a desk, leather armchairs, and a carpet. It looked more like a private study than an office.

The man behind the desk was medium height, plump, in his late fifties. His uniform was smart, awash with glitter. He had neat grey hair and a slender moustache. His eyes were inclined to protrude, as if he were willing to be startled.

The chief constable, whom Cartland considered to be an amiable fool, spent half his time in London. He was fond of chorus girls and driving while drunk. His position he owed less to ability than to a family connexion with the county's lord lieutenant.

The formality of greetings over, the men sat down. Cartland began to talk about the autopsy on Mrs. Lunn, which had added nothing to the doctor's preliminary examination.

The chief constable said, "Yes, Inspector. Quite. But is the case still open? The tramp, y'know."

"Certainly the case is still open, sir."

"Suicide. Must be your man, appears to me."

"I don't see that it follows, sir."

"Why else would he kill himself?"

Jack Cartland felt again what he had experienced on first hearing of the death: guilt. Was it his threatening the man with a murder charge that had led him to take his life?

Earnestly talking as much for his own benefit as the other man's, Cartland said:

"He was a down-and-out. There wasn't a penny on. He may have been planning suicide anyway, could have been about to do it when our lads caught him. His prints aren't in the house. It's unlikely he had anything to do with the murder. He ended his life because it wasn't worth living."

"Oh well. I suppose. Perhaps. And then there's the matter of the suicide itself."

"How do you mean, sir?"

"You know, man in custody. There'll be talk of negligence."

Cartland sighed. "We took all the usual precautions—pockets emptied, cords and belts and shoelaces removed. We couldn't possibly know he'd have razor blades in the lining of his coat."

"That's very true."

"The turnkey thought he was sleeping. The blood from his wrists soaked into the mattress, didn't run on the floor where it could be seen. If the court starts accusing the police . . ."

"No, no," the chief constable said. "There'll be none of that. I'll have a word with Harry."

He was referring to the coroner, who operated a market garden.

Cartland subsided with a grumbled, "All right."

"So the case is still open, Inspector?"

"Yes, sir. We want a murder weapon. We want to know

what she was doing there. We want the killer. And we'll get him."

"What procedures are you taking?"

Cartland knew it was a waste of time to go into detail: the house-to-house checks, enquiries into the Lunns's background, all the mechanics of an investigation.

He said, "The usual lines, sir."

"Do you think we should call in Scotland Yard?"

The inspector gave him a hard stare. In it there was a flicker of fear. "I do not. I certainly do not. There's no sense in bringing in strangers. I know the ground. I know the people."

The chief constable winced and blinked, as if intimidated. "Exactly my view," he said.

"Good."

"Is there anything else, Inspector?"

Downstairs, still taut, Jack Cartland was about to head straight for the door when he saw the sergeant silently waving. With his other hand he held a telephone receiver to his face.

He mouthed elaborately, "Listen on the extension."

Cartland quickly circled the counter, went to a desk, and picked up a telephone. He heard:

". . . I can tell you, I'm afraid. Perhaps it means nothing, but I thought you'd better be told, just in case."

The voice was male.

"Fine, sir," the sergeant said. "We appreciate your help. Now would you like to go over it once again, please. See if I've got it straight."

"About ten o'clock the night before last, I was driving along the road past Gorse Manor. I passed a man who was either getting on or off a bicycle, sort of poised there. He was tall and fairly young. I wouldn't recognise him again."

"Fine. Sure you wouldn't care to identify yourself, sir?"

"I'd rather not get involved. Good morning."

Jack Cartland lowered the receiver. He went back around the counter. "What do you reckon, Sam? Genuine?"

The sergeant nodded. "I'd say so. He sounded calm and reasonable."

"And fairly educated and about forty, maybe younger. The age matters. What does *fairly young* mean to a man of forty?"

"Could mean twenty. On the other hand, Jack, if he's a vain type, he could be referring to someone his own age."

Cartland nodded with appreciation. "That's shrewd, Sam. You'll get to be a sergeant yet."

"Ta."

"See you later."

Out on the street, Cartland paused to consider his next move. He noticed that several passers-by looked his way with recognition. It pleased him.

A car stopped on the other side of the street. The driver was one of the London reporters.

Jack Cartland went back inside the doorway. From its dimness he watched the journalist get out of the car and come across the road. When he was almost at the doorway, Cartland stepped out briskly and began to stride away.

"Hold on, Super!" the reporter said, grabbing his arm.

He was an untidy man of thirty, with urgent eyes, curly hair, and whisky-smelling breath. His suit, though new and stylishly nipped in at the waist, bespoke the cheapest ready-made rack. He reminded Cartland of an unsuccessful pimp.

He asked, "What's the big hurry, Super?"

"Inspector."

"Great. Where you going?"

"New line of enquiry," Cartland said. "Could be something of consequence."

The reporter looked skeptical. "Yes? Sure the case isn't over?"

"Of course it isn't."

"Seems to me it died with the tramp. You know, could be he was having it off with Mrs. Lunn."

"That's not very likely."

The reporter became confidential. "Listen, chief. Between you and me and the gatepost, how hot is Harold Lunn as a suspect?"

Bland of face, the inspector said, "I am not at liberty to make a statement on that. Now excuse me, please. This is important.". He walked off swiftly.

Around the first corner he slowed, made sure he wasn't being followed, and went in search of a newspaper shop. Finding one, he bought copies of the national dailies. Later, in other shops, he would buy repeats.

After calling headquarters from a telephone box and ordering a car to be ready in twenty minutes, he went into a tea room and sat over tea and a sandwich while reading the papers at his leisure.

The people at the table behind him, a man and woman, were talking about the murder. He listened, smiling, to their retailing of misinformation.

Rising to leave, the man said, "Lunn did it, bet you what you like."

The woman said, "Nothing of the kind. I can just imagine what the poor soul's going through."

Cartland felt depressed. He had not looked at the murder from that angle. He had given Harold Lunn verbal, formal sympathy while feeling no such emotion. If Lunn was innocent, he had pain. Cartland knew all about that. He still ached.

The inspector straightened his spine. This, he told himself, was dangerous thinking. Grossly unprofessional. It was like a nurse saying this is going to hurt so I won't do it.

He got up to leave.

Ten minutes later he was at the house in Piper Street. His knock was answered by a man, tall and youthful. His face had the stamp of openness.

"Mr. Michael Shield?"

"Yes."

"Inspector Cartland, CID."

The young man nodded. "I've been expecting you. Come in, please."

The house was neat and pleasant, but its ambience had a deadness, an indefinable quality of lack.

The men sat in armchairs siding the fire. Conversationally, Jack Cartland asked, "Mr. Lunn's out?"

"Funeral arrangements. He has a lot to do."

"He must be taking this pretty hard."

Shield leaned forward over clasped hands. "It's been a great shock," he said.

Tall, Inspector Cartland was thinking. Tall and fairly young.

He said, "Well, Mr. Shield, let's get down to business. As you know, I'm investigating the death of Mrs. Lunn."

"Yes."

"I'm hoping you can help me on one or two points."

"Inspector," Shield said, "I'll be very happy to give you all the help I can."

His manner was so innocent, child-like, so earnest, that Cartland felt a mite foolish for the implication behind his first question:

"What was your relationship with Mrs. Lunn?"

"Friendly. We were on very good terms."

"You were together a lot?"

"For hours every day. We were extremely close."

"You were fond of her then."

"Oh yes. She was a wonderful person."

"And beautiful."

The young man nodded. "Beautiful."

Beautiful and glamorous and sophisticated, Jack Cartland thought. Would she be interested in this naïve, unattractive lad? Hardly.

"It's been suggested, Mr. Shield, simply as a possibility, that you and Mrs. Lunn were romantically involved."

"Oh?"

"Could that be?"

The young man looked uncomfortable. "I—I really don't know, Inspector."

His manner, Cartland thought, could be interpreted as "It's not true but I wouldn't mind if it were believed to be."

"No flirting? An affair, perhaps? These things do happen."

Shield shook his head, looking down.

"Okay then," Cartland said. "Maybe you can tell me how the Lunns got on together."

"Very well indeed."

"A love match?"

Shield looked up. "Yes, I think so. Yes."

"They must have quarrelled, of course. All couples do."

"Not so far as I know. They were happy."

Jack Cartland smiled to show friendliness, the man-to-man approach. "If you were in my place, would you suspect Harold Lunn?"

Shield's face was blank. "Suspect him of what?"

"Of killing his wife."

The blankness was replaced by an expression of shock. The inspector would have bet heavily that it was genuine.

He asked, "No?"

"Oh no. Never. Not Mr. Lunn."

"There are indications, you see, that we have to check. His fingerprints were found in the house—though that's between you and me. He claims he was there a week ago."

Shield nodded. The eagerness was back. "I remember that. Rosalind—Mrs. Lunn—she told me he'd said he was going there."

Could be true, Cartland thought. Could also be true he was trying to help Lunn.

"The night of the murder, Mr. Shield. Did you go out?"

"No."

"Do you own a car?"

"No. I can't drive."

"Bicycle?"

"Yes, I have a bike. I like cycling."

"Did anyone call here that night?"

"No. I was alone. I read."

Just a simple lad, Cartland mused. He brought out note-book and pencil, feeling the approach of boredom. "Well, Mr. Shield," he said, "if you can just give me a few details about your background, we'll call it a day."

The police car was on the edge of the town centre, in one of Stilton's seamier districts. The street lighting threw garish, offensive patches of yellow. The shops were small and mean. Two ragged drunks supported one another in a doorway.

Some way ahead of the car, a small crowd was gathered outside a public house. Watching closely, the inspector gave the car more speed. It was an instinctive, professional reaction.

"Looks like trouble," he said, speaking aloud although he was actually talking to himself.

The other three in the car watched out of politeness, each tight-held within himself.

Drawing level, slowing, Inspector Cartland saw that the crowd was passive, even listless. Some people found it more rewarding to turn their attention on the passing car, away from the primary object, a man and a woman having a fumbled argument.

Cartland put his foot down on the accelerator.

"Some folk will watch anything," he said, and remembered how on the first day of the investigation a crowd had gathered at the Gorse Manor gatehouse to stare pointlessly up the driveway.

Hearing of this, he had sent a constable to scatter the

gawkers. Telephoning from the gatehouse, the constable had reported that the job had already been done skillfully by the caretaker. Her sharp tongue had jabbed everyone away.

Cartland laughed shortly. He related the incident to the other occupants of the car, finishing, "She kept it up, too, that Mrs. Trent."

"You'd think people'd have something better to do," Mrs. Foster said.

"Unpleasant," Michael Shield murmured.

Harold Lunn, throwing a cigarette end out of the window, said, "Something similar happened to me."

The inspector gave him a glance. "You should've reported it. We don't stand for nonsense like that."

"Luckily, I didn't hear about it until later. A neighbour told me. He said people were suddenly finding it convenient to walk along Piper Street, and dawdle when they came opposite my house—for some reason they never walked on my side of the street."

Mrs. Foster: "Horrible."

Harold Lunn went on, "At one point, apparently, there were twenty people bunching up and pretending not to see each other. There were cars as well, crawling by, and bikes."

Leaning forward, Mrs. Foster put her hand on his shoulder. She said, "What you've been through this past week, Mr. Lunn."

He closed his eyes.

———————◆———————

Rosalind had been dead for three days. Harold had come to accept the fact of her death and was growing accustomed to his omnipresent feeling of melancholy. Recovery, he knew, was being aided by the existence of other problems.

Apart from all the dreary details attendant upon a life ended, there were reporters to avoid and the suspicions of the police to fight.

Harold, sitting in his office, chain smoking, had just returned from a second interview with Inspector Cartland. They had gone over the same ground as before. However, whereas during that first talk suspicion had been muffled, now it was out in the open. It had been more like the third degree of gangster movies than an interview.

Cartland had come right out with the question, "Did you kill your wife?"

"I did not."

"Then what were you doing in the area that night?"

"I wasn't there."

"You followed her in your car, parked it, and went the rest of the way on foot. You were seen."

That had been a terrifying moment. But it came to him while making vehement denials that the policeman must be bluffing, otherwise there would be a confrontation with the observer. An observer there might have been, but he or she could not have had a close look. Which didn't mean others might not come forward.

Harold lit another cigarette, got up to pace his office briefly, sat again. He was afraid.

The police could well build up a circumstantial case, he mused. They had talked to all his friends about him and Rosalind. They had asked questions at every house in Piper Street. They had gone again—two young detectives—to Mrs. Foster's to try and break her story. In time she might give in.

Harold ran his mind away from that possibility.

Reporters, he thought. A blot on the face of the earth. They had waited like vultures outside the house, they had telephoned time after time, they had tried to force their way into the office, and had even attempted to buy "information" from one of the junior clerks. The local boys were fairly reticent, but those four men from London—scum.

They suspected the worst, which for them meant the best: respected citizen murders wife. And they weren't the only ones who suspected, along with the police. One acquaintance had cut him in the street. Wherever he went people whispered and pointed. The telephone—

Harold started violently, his mouth in an upcurling twist, as the telephone at his elbow gave a shrill ring.

Settling, taking a deep breath, he lifted the receiver. "Yes?"

"Could I speak to Mr. Lunn, please?" a female voice asked.

"Who's calling?"

"I can't give you a name. I just want to talk to him."

Another one, Harold thought. He said, "Mr. Lunn is out for the day. Good morning."

The voice snapped, "Well, I'd like you to know—"

Harold put the receiver down.

There had been eight calls, some at home, some to the office. All were anonymous. Seven had called him a murderer, either in a sly and roundabout way or so directly as to be obscene. One caller had said, "Chin up, mate. They'll get the right man sooner or later." That call had reduced him to tears.

Sighing, Harold looked down at the newspapers on his desk. Again he felt relief on noting that the case had got no bigger. Although it was maintaining its position on the front pages of the national dailies, it was still fourth or fifth lead. It did form the headline story of the Stilton paper, but that was to be expected. The case was the most sensational happening locally for years.

Which, Harold consoled himself, accounted for the viciousness and gossip. People were stirred by excitement, not by a genuine conviction of his guilt. It was a sort of mob madness.

Harold sat on in his office, attempting no work, distraught with his companions of sorrow and fear, until close to 11 A.M. He left the building by the back door.

A series of alleys brought him to a street on which stood the town hall, the council chamber of which was being used for the inquest.

The street was crowded.

Harold stayed in the alley's mouth. There must be four or five hundred people, he reckoned. They were massed in front of the town hall as quietly as if attending a funeral. Their quiet was uncanny.

On the steps of the building, two constables stood guard. They turned back a woman who made as though to enter, then a man.

The public gallery is full, Harold mused grimly. All seats for the show are taken. So what is everyone waiting for? The star turn, of course. Dr. Jekyll and Mr. Hyde, alias the Lunn twins.

Nervously, Harold moved his eyes over the crowd. He was not conscious of the fact that he was looking for reassuring signs. He saw none.

What he did see was many familiar faces, people he had known casually or well all his life. Some were losing valuable work time by being here. It was absurd, and sick.

One man he noticed was a neighbour from Piper Street. The manager of a furniture store, he had a wife and two young children.

Absurd, Harold thought.

Then he looked back at the man, who was tall, good-looking, and aged about thirty. Their last meeting had been at a New Year's Eve party.

Harold felt a pulse of excitement. John McKay and Rosalind had danced together a lot, more times than had seemed proper. The same had happened at a party on Boxing Day. He hadn't minded, and might not have given it a second thought except for the look of annoyance on Mrs. McKay's face.

Harold suddenly recalled another incident. His pulse beat faster.

At that New Year's Eve party, the group had started playing children's games, which, surprisingly, had been fun: spin the bottle, musical chairs, postman's knock. It was during the last that, as part of the game, Rosalind and John McKay were out of the room together, McKay to collect his kiss tribute. As often happens, someone flung open the door. There the couple were, locked together in a passionate-looking kiss. Everyone laughed uproariously. Harold laughed as well. Then.

And now?

He wondered if he were being misled by panic. There had been other dancing partners, she had been out of the room with more than just McKay, other men had kissed her with gusto, under the mistletoe. John McKay was one possibility, and he happened to have been here now, conveniently.

But the lover must be *someone*, Harold thought. It was time he gave his mind to that, stopped fretting about himself.

The town hall clock began to strike.

The crowd murmured.

Harold waited until the tenth, penultimate clang of the bell. He left the alley and walked along the street. Slowly, he edged through the crowd. Behind him he left ripples of whispered comment like waves behind a boat. They spread. People ahead turned to look back. He went on, his face stony, a lifeless figurehead. Comment dipped and swelled, heads bobbed. Harold felt nauseated.

He reached the steps and went quickly up. The constables let him by. He walked a dim passage and through a doorway guarded by another policeman.

He had seen the council chamber often. It was circular, with tiers of seats rising from the well and ending close to the domed ceiling. A hundred years before, it had been used as a cock-pit and for dog fights.

Behind the high bench were the flags of nation, county, and town, flanking a portrait of the new king, George VI. The mayor's mace of office had been moved to one side of the bench; it looked like a threat under the present circumstances: an ornate bludgeon.

The chamber was crowded. Harold kept his gaze down as

he moved to where he had been told he should sit—in the well of the court. A dozen other men were there. One was Inspector Cartland. He and Harold exchanged nods. There was antagonism on both sides.

Harold felt that he and the policeman were like a pair of Staffordshire bull-terriers, about to do battle to the death.

The coroner appeared behind the bench. The inquest began.

Listening to the droning voices, Harold shared his gaze among the floor, the face of the coroner, and those of the six-man jury.

His own giving of evidence was not as traumatic as he had expected. The questions were concise and familiar. He answered in a clear voice which rang around the chamber. He stood tall. Yet he was sweating as he returned to his seat.

Next came the doctor, in his morning dress.

Harold closed his mind to the medical evidence. He couldn't bear to think about what had happened to his lovely Rosalind at the hospital.

He went back over his own session in the witness box. The name which had recurred most was Gorse Manor. It formed the second biggest mystery of the case, after the killer's identity: What had Mrs. Lunn been doing there? His own allaying theory had received a cool reception, he felt. It wasn't bizarre enough. The idea of a prank reduced the drama. It didn't fit with the story of James Gorse.

Harold thought of that story.

Gorse was a self-made man. The son of a farmhand, he had started a feed mill in a derelict building. There was no sudden success. He had turned forty before he accumulated enough to buy another mill, the second of an eventual chain of twenty, and to start construction of his dream house. When, after six years, Gorse Manor was finished, James Gorse moved in with as many of his family as were willing to accept his hospitality.

Gorse was a fiery little man. He had a bristly moustache,

hard eyes, and stumping, fast movements. He was a martinet. Since his wife's death, he had given all his affection to his only grandchild. Amelia's mother and her two aunts he had no time for, nor for their husbands, his sons-in-law, whom he considered fortune-hunting wastrels and whom his daughters had married against his wishes.

Nevertheless, Gorse was willing to have them all under his roof. He enjoyed being a despot, he loved to make the six adults respect his whims and strict morality and abstemiousness, and he adored the constant company of Amelia.

Fearful of disinheritance, the daughters and their husbands stayed on. They sublimated their desire for a lively life by developing an active hate for their keeper, also resentment for the child he loved and indulged.

The house had an unfortunate atmosphere. Servants came and went continually, in particular Amelia's governesses, who were upset by a confusion of orders in respect of the child.

When Amelia was eight years old, Gorse was forced to go away for a time. He disliked leaving her and the comfort of home, but his Scottish mill had developed problems.

As soon as the trap was out of sight, on its way to the railway station, the family gave a groan of relief and opened a bottle of champagne. It was to be the first of several hundred.

Friends were sent for, two cousins came, selected acquaintances in town were urged to attend as often as they wished. The celebration was practically non-stop. Years of frustration were being attacked viciously with laughter and wine, dancing and libertinism. To the moral climate of the times, it was a disgusting Bacchanalia.

Amelia was ignored, servants left and were not replaced, Stilton's vintners arrived almost daily with new supplies. Two months had passed since James Gorse left for Scotland, and the festivities showed no signs of abating.

The last servant was the governess. She had stayed this

long out of kindliness toward the neglected child. Following an attempt at seduction by one of the sons-in-law, she left, slipping away quietly at first light. Amelia awoke and tried to catch her up, running barefoot across the estate. Unsuccessful, she returned soaked from the dew.

Two days later Amelia had a high fever. No one noticed. The family, either in various stages of drunkenness or sick recovery from drunkenness, barely noticed that the girl's personal servant had gone.

Sloppy and disorganised, the revels continued. Cousins and friends drifted away. The house became filthy.

This was the state of things when James Gorse, apprised of the situation by the last governess, returned unexpectedly to his home.

He found the family sitting over a makeshift breakfast in the dining room; they stared at him stupidly. Upstairs, he found Amelia in a coma.

Gorse rushed out and ran to town. He came back with Stilton's three doctors. They worked over Amelia all day. She died as the full moon began to rise.

James Gorse had been waiting tensely in his study. Consumed with concern for his grandchild, he had not yet spoken to the family, who sat fearfully in the hall below.

Told the news, Gorse strode out onto the gallery. He lurched into a paroxysm of rage and sorrow, alternately weeping and shrieking abuse. It lasted for minutes. He beat his brow, he thudded his fists on the balustrade, he leaned over into dangerous tilts in his screamed condemnation of those below.

Drooping and drooling at last into a state of comparative normalcy, he said hoarsely, pointing:

"I curse you. I curse all of you. You will never know a moment's happiness. Whatever you wish will be denied you. Everyone in this house—"

He broke off, turned, and staggered back into the study. He collapsed there. An hour later, he died.

The family drifted away within days of the double funeral. They were never heard of again. No one locally knew which member had arranged for a stone likeness of Amelia to be made and placed on the front lawn, nor did anyone know if this appeasement had helped.

Over the years the stories of hauntings grew, and changed, and were exaggerated: headless men, screaming women in trailing gowns, crying children. No reliable person, however, could be found to lay claim to having witnessed these phenomena. The occasional tenants of Gorse Manor never put name to . . .

Harold Lunn looked up.

He had been brought back to his surroundings by a palpable change in the atmosphere. He saw that during his mental absence the jury had been sent out. Now the six men were returning.

Harold sat straighter. He fixed his eyes on the first juryman, who remained standing while the others sat. The man seemed embarrassed on account of his prominence, like a boy called out in front of the class.

The coroner asked, "Have you reached a verdict?"

"Yes, sir. Murder by a person or persons unknown."

A mumble of desultory talk arose from the court. Unconcerned by the verdict, which was the expected one, Harold looked at his watch. The inquest had taken less than an hour.

"Yes," a voice said. "They were quick about it."

Inspector Cartland was lowering himself into the chair next to Harold's. "Bit of a record for a coroner's jury."

"Yes."

"Out six minutes."

"They had nothing much to thresh out," Harold said. "Only the question of that tramp. You were certainly firm in your refusal to accept him as the murderer."

Inspector Cartland folded his big arms and leaned closer. "You've never pressed him as a candidate yourself. Which is odd."

"You're the investigator."

"Sure you don't know something you've—er—forgotten to mention?"

"Don't be coy, Inspector," Harold said coldly.

A ripple of displeasure moved over the policeman's face. Tightening the grip of his folded arms, as if giving an invisible enemy a bear-hug, he asked:

"Remember what Dr. Patcher said about the most likely weapon being a hammer?"

Harold lied, "Yes."

"Well, it occurred to me we might have been searching in all the wrong places."

"Which means?"

The inspector looked at him closely. "We haven't yet searched your house, Mr. Lunn."

Harold didn't like the penetrating stare. He turned his eyes away, saying, "If I were the killer, I'd hardly be stupid enough to keep the murder weapon in a drawer at home."

Harold stiffened. A shock ran through him that made his legs twitch.

Rosalind's diary, he thought. Christ.

"Could have been put there by someone else," the policeman was saying. "To incriminate you."

Shock made Harold get to his feet. He moved a step away, trying to compose his face. The court was now empty apart from Cartland and himself.

The inspector said, "I'd like to go to your house and look around, if you don't mind."

Harold took a quietly deep breath and turned. "I do mind," he said, snapping the words.

"Why?"

"Why not?"

Cartland smiled. "An innocent man wouldn't mind, Mr. Lunn."

"An innocent man would have nothing to gain by what you *wouldn't* find."

"You refuse to co-operate?"

"Yes."

"That's bad."

"So be it."

The inspector stood up. He was no longer smiling. He said, "Whether you like it or not, I'm going to search your house. You've made me determined. If it's necessary, I can get a warrant within two hours."

"Get one."

Cartland slanted his head. "A search warrant being needed will look black for you."

"Let it," Harold said. "Good day."

Shoulders straight, he walked out of the chamber. He made himself move at a normal pace. The desire to run was an ache.

Outside, the body of the crowd had gone. Only groups of two and three remained. These broke off talk to stare as Harold crossed the street. From one group came a loud:

"Well, one thing's sure, the tramp didn't do it."

Entering the alley, Harold went at a smart stride, heading for the rear of his office where the car was parked.

In seven minutes he was driving along Piper Street. He jerked to a stop, got out, and went quickly into the house, not even pausing to close the front door.

Running upstairs, he flung into the bedroom he had shared with Rosalind, crossed to the chest, and dragged open a lower drawer.

The diary was there. Holding it with both hands, he went downstairs. A fire smouldered greyly in the living-room hearth. Harold sank to his knees by the grate. He lifted the poker and jabbed at the feebly glowing coals. There was little effect.

Placing the book open, roof-like on the fire, he got matches off the mantel and set flame to the pages.

There was a noise in the hallway.

His hand shaking, Harold got the tongs. He began to take

coals from the fire's edge and put them atop the diary. They slid off its back.

The door opened.

Harold jerked around. He shuddered on seeing the mild person of Michael Shield.

"I'm busy," he said faintly.

The boarder came farther into the room. He leaned to look around Harold at the fire.

"I didn't bother to build it up," he said. "It's a warm day."

Harold turned back. The diary was flaming well on its underside.

Shield asked in a conversational tone, "What's that you're burning, Mr. Lunn?"

"Nothing."

"Why, it's a book," the boarder said. He sounded shocked.

"Listen. It's nothing. It's about the occult. I've finished with all that."

Could he risk asking the young man to forget what he had seen?

Harold was suddenly exhausted. The tension, which had made him so, now left, as if satisfied with its work. Slowly he got to his feet and turned. He no longer cared.

"Mr. Shield," he said quietly. "There's not much point in your staying on here. You've been very good about making your own meals and so forth, and I thank you for that. I suggest you find a hotel until you can make other arrangements."

The boarder nodded absently, his gaze on the fire. He looked unhappy. "Yes, all right."

"Fix up a place today and move tomorrow. If you don't mind."

"No, that's fine."

Harold said, "I'll be going back to the office in a minute. Inspector Cartland will probably show up here with a search warrant. It's all right. Let him in."

"Yes. And there's the rent. I owe from last—"

"Forget it," Harold said, turning away. "Forget it."

He heard the door close and then Michael Shield's footfalls on the stairs.

Putting his hands on the mantel, Harold sagged into a lean and watched the diary being corroded by flames. He stayed thus until there was nothing but a black twisted semblance of the original.

With the tongs he lifted pieces of the carbon to the flue's top and let them be drawn up by the draught. This he continued, though slowly, not wanting to litter the sky with floating debris, until the fireplace was clear of paper.

He went out and drove back to town.

The afternoon Harold spent in his office was uninterrupted: the chief clerk had orders to that effect, especially in regard of telephone calls.

Harold's thoughts played one theme—John McKay. Harold became more and more positive that he had picked the right man. He searched for, and found, other incidents in addition to those of the holiday season: chats which went on too long, a stroll together at a picnic, other party kisses, Rosalind's poor opinion of McKay's wife.

If McKay was the lover, Harold mused, then he was the one who had met her at Gorse Manor, therefore the apparent murderer. But what could be done about it?

Harold also wondered if he wanted it made public that his wife had been another man's mistress. He decided he didn't. Except as a last resort, to save himself.

At four o'clock he telephoned John McKay at his furniture store. Could they get together later for a drink, about seven at the Crown and Anchor? McKay was reluctant.

"It's not important," Harold said, retreating to victory. "I'm feeling a bit lonely, that's all."

McKay said, "I'll be there at seven, Harry."

Harold rang off with a humourless smile. He had always loathed the diminutive of his name. Somehow, that made John McKay more fitting for the role of lover-killer.

The afternoon post was brought in by a junior. All the letters were business save one, marked "Personal," which was the only one Harold opened. Unsigned, it called him a butcher and a mad animal that should be exterminated.

Harold threw it in the waste-paper basket.

He was the last to leave the office at five-thirty. He went out the back way. He was turning out of the yard when a man stepped in front of him.

Harold halted quickly with a nervous uplift of his arms. He frowned on recognising the man. He was the London reporter who always looked and smelled half drunk.

He asked, smiling, "And how is Mr. Harold Lunn?"

"No better for seeing you."

"Would he care to comment to the press on the fact that his house was searched this afternoon, by warrant?"

Partly to himself, Harold said, "So he did it."

The journalist flapped open a newspaper and held it in front of him like a tract. It was Stilton's *Evening News*. The headline said "Police Search Lunn Home." There was a picture of Inspector Cartland leaving the house.

Lightly, Harold asked, "Did they find my confession?"

"I gather he thought it odd there was no hammer in the coal shed."

Harold snorted. "Good God."

The reporter said, "Well, Mr. Harold Lunn should realise that *everyone* has a coal hammer."

"We buy the best Newcastle cobs. They don't need breaking."

"Mmm."

Why the hell am I standing here talking to this idiot sot? Harold thought. He pushed past roughly and walked on.

The reporter called out, "Why did your wife dye her hair last year?"

When Harold was in the car and driving, he smiled, Yes, why did she?

The answering thought was: John McKay's wife has very

light-coloured hair. Perhaps he has a passion for blondes.

In a grimy, dim pub on the outskirts of town, Harold ate cheese sandwiches as thick as shoes and drank mild beer. He was the sole customer. The landlady gave him only passing, disinterested glances. Leaving, he sat in the car until seven o'clock.

The Crown and Anchor lay between Piper Street and the centre of town. It was a large pub with the usual two rooms— sawdusty saloon for caps and mufflers, carpeted lounge for collars and ties.

The talk from the half-dozen people in the lounge lessened in volume as Harold entered. Face wooden, he stood at an empty stretch of bar and ordered a scotch. He was aware of lingering scrutiny. Although he told himself he didn't care, he was glad when his neighbour came in.

John McKay was athletically built. He wore his clothes well. He had brown curly hair, a coarsely handsome face, and an easy manner. There was something of the matinée idol about him.

The men shook hands, muttered commonplaces. Harold bought another whisky and a beer for McKay. They moved to a table and sat.

Harold said, "Thanks for the letter of sympathy, by the way."

"I wish there was something more we could do. Jane and I were both fond of Rosalind."

"All I need, John, is to find out who killed her. For selfish reasons. As you must be aware, I'm the chief suspect."

"It's all nonsense, Harry."

"Yes, but it's getting me down, this suspicion. I can't prove I didn't do it."

"You don't have to."

Harold stubbed out his cigarette and took a sip of whisky. He said, "The trouble is, my alibi isn't perfect. The time of death is pretty vague. Most people would find it difficult proving they were somewhere else when Rosalind was killed."

"Yes."

"For example, yourself. If the police came to you, would you be able to give them an alibi?"

John McKay lit a cigarette. His hands were steady. He blew out smoke and said, "I was at home reading."

"Witnesses?"

"Jane was in bed. She had a cold, went to bed early. The children were asleep as well."

Harold spread his hands. "You see? The police would say you left the house, met Rosalind at Gorse Manor, killed her, and returned home."

John McKay looked uncomfortable. "They might if they had any reason to suspect me, or whoever the person is who can't give a good alibi."

"They'd think of something. They'd say you and Rosalind were having an affair."

Harold was watching intently for the reaction. It was a disappointment. McKay merely nodded, drained his glass, and stood up. "What're you having, Harry?"

"Scotch, please."

McKay went to the bar. Despite the poor response, Harold's conviction was growing that he had made the right choice. That lack of alibi was the green light.

When McKay returned with fresh drinks, Harold said, "I'm not without hope, as it happens."

"Er—hope?"

"That the police will find the right man."

"Of course."

"That tramp who killed himself. Inspector Cartland told me in the strictest confidence that, in a statement he made, he gave a good description of a man he'd seen inside the house that night."

McKay's expression showed only interest. "Really?"

"Yes. He was in the house, that tramp, intended sleeping

there, in a room by the foot of the stairs. He heard a noise and came to the door and saw the man coming across the hall."

"Well, there you are. That should let you out. If the description doesn't fit."

Did he imagine it or had McKay's voice taken on a different edge and his words a new sharpness?

"Cartland said something about disguise. But, of course, they're still looking. There are others under suspicion but Cartland hasn't said who they are."

McKay took a drink.

Harold went on, "He did say the man was probably Rosalind's lover, in his opinion."

"Do you go along with that?" John McKay asked, getting out another cigarette.

"I don't know any more. I—"

Harold broke off and snapped his fingers. He produced an expression of pleased surprise. "By God," he said.

"What is it, Harry?"

"The police searched my house today. I thought they were wasting their time. But I've just remembered. There was something that might give them the whole answer. They must have found it."

McKay had struck a match. He took the cigarette from his mouth, blew out the match, and asked:

"What? What did they find?

"Rosalind's diary!" Harold said as if announcing a happy event.

"Oh."

"I'd forgotten all about it. She put everything in there. *Everything.* Names, dates, the works. If she did have a lover, his name'll be in the diary."

McKay nodded. He struck another match and lit his cigarette. His hands still appeared to be steady.

He said, "Let's hope so. Let's hope it gets cleared up soon. You're under a hell of a strain, Harry."

"Don't worry. I'm holding together."

McKay lifted his glass and looked over at the wall clock. "Well, must hurry off to home and hearth."

When John McKay had gone, Harold got himself a double whisky. As he sipped it, his spirits oozed down from the high point, slowly, like a mound of ice cream in the sun.

What, he wondered, had he accomplished with his bluffs re the tramp and the diary? Nothing. Unless McKay disappeared from home, or out of fear made some sort of mistake. It would have been better to say the diary was hidden where it couldn't have been found, and, yes, and that he was now on his way to tell the police about it. McKay might then have shown his hand.

Depressed, Harold finished the whisky and got another. He continued drinking until the pub closed.

Outside, he reeled. He suddenly felt drunk. Leaving the car, he set off walking, face starkly grim as he strove for sobriety and steadiness. He tacked slovenly, like an old horse on a hill.

Once he heard the sound of youthful laughter, but didn't look around for fear of breaking into the concentration he was using to walk. He felt desperate and alone.

The house was silent, the fire dead. Harold went into the kitchen in search of a drink. Behind the door he saw Rosalind's striped apron. He fingered it wonderingly. He took it down, wrapped it around his neck, and lurched into the living room. Falling onto the couch, he covered his head with the apron and began to sob.

Next thing he knew, the room was attackingly bright with morning.

Shakily, he washed in the kitchen, drank three glasses of water, swallowed aspirins for the pain in his head. Not bothering to shave, he left the house.

He got his car and drove to work. When his clerks began to arrive, he sent one of them out for tea and sandwiches.

After breakfast he telephoned the furniture store and

asked for John McKay. A voice said, "Speaking." Harold lowered the receiver.

Until ten, he sat steeped in misery.

His head clerk came in. "Sir, there's a man on the telephone. He won't give a name but he sounds different from the others."

"All right."

The clerk left and Harold lifted the receiver: "Harold Lunn here."

"Morning." The voice was gruff. "I don't know if you know this, but people're saying you killed your missus with a hammer what you bought on a stall at the market two weeks back."

"No, I didn't know."

"There *was* a man bought a hammer. It was one a them small thick ones with a square top. He acted funny-like. But I saw that man and he wasn't you. I know you, Mr. Lunn. I've seen you here and there. It wasn't you. And I know you wouldn't kill your missus anyway."

Harold put a hand to his throat, which felt tight. "Thank you," he said. "Thank you."

———————◄◆►———————

The police car moved through suburban streets at a strict, legal thirty miles an hour. Now that the town centre had been left behind, there were few people about. Dampness slicked the road in odd, illogical patches and formed glitter on trees.

Her lined and kindly face set so tautly that it quivered with the car's every bump and sway, Mrs. Foster was sitting back in the seat, pressed hard against the upholstery. Her hands were tightly clasped. Minute by minute, her tension was growing.

She said, almost gasped, "It's not far now." She was reassuring herself.

Harold Lunn looked back, giving a one-sided smile that appeared to be caused by a twinge of pain. "A couple of miles," he said. "Not long." Facing the front again, he drew deeply on his cigarette.

He could understand Mrs. Foster's feelings. He was the same himself. It was now or never. Harold wished the inspector wouldn't dawdle so.

Michael Shield sat leaning forward, his hands on the back of the seat in front. His eyes were unblinking, he wore a faint smile.

The interior of the car was abruptly flooded with harsh light: headlights charging up to the rear. The glare grew to an affront, then swung away.

The car behind drew level, and, with an imperious blast on the horn, swept past. It was travelling at more than double the speed limit.

Inspector Cartland grunted, officially and personally. He grunted again on noting that the racing vehicle ahead was a Rolls Royce.

Someone of consequence, he thought; power. Which made the fact of law-breaking worse. It was a disgusting abuse of position. Gross dishonesty.

But, came the snide question, was he himself, in respect of position, always perfectly honest?

He tried to escape the thought by dwelling on how curious, coincidental, it was because of tonight that the Rolls Royce was the Silver Ghost model.

And, not escaping, he returned to the question, which was particularised now as, Had he been honest at the inquest on Mrs. Lunn?

Shuffling uncomfortably, Jack Cartland once more attempted a deflecting ploy. He told himself he had been quite right to keep the tramp's part in the drama to a minimum. Smith had been uninvolved.

That wasn't it at all, Cartland thought sourly. It was the mantelshelf. Why hadn't he mentioned the mantelshelf? He should at least have offered it as being, in reception, a possible instrument of death, the mute assassin.

His answer to himself was, Too many other things to worry about. Far too many to bother with remote, stupid possibilities.

Sternly, he pressed his foot down on the accelerator. The car's speed built up to forty.

———◆———

"All right, Mr. Lunn," the inspector said into the telephone. "I'll follow it up. Yes. Leave it to me. 'Bye."

Lowering the receiver to its cradle with the precision of inattentiveness, he said, "Well, well, well."

Detective Tarkinson was leaning on the wall by the door. He asked, "Is Lunn taking a crank call seriously?"

"Interesting."

"You should have told him how many we've had, sir, and how many man hours we've wasted checking them out." He shook his head. "My poor feet."

Cartland leaned forward on his desk and put one bloated hand atop the other.

"Interesting," he said. "If it's a real lead, why didn't the man call us? And why didn't he give his name? And why didn't he describe the buyer? . . . Just saying it wasn't Harold Lunn is a fat lot of good."

"Except for Harold Lunn."

"Could be all his own work, in fact. It could be he's throwing us a red herring. That's what's really interesting about it."

"Yes, sir," the detective said. "If he's going in for this kind of stuff, he must be getting worried."

"That could be it, yes. We'll see."

The detective eased himself away from the wall. "We're not going to check on his story, are we?"

"Nothing else to do," the inspector said. "We haven't got a lead worth a damn. There was nothing in the Lunn house, the dead Smith still has no other identity, we've got no weapon, no one's said anything useful about Lunn's relationship with his wife or her relationship with anyone else. So we might as well check."

"Oh well."

Cartland heaved himself up and came around the desk. "Don't look so full of joy, son. I'll handle this one."

Outside, away from the police station, Inspector Cartland slowed his stride. He lost some of the bearing he had maintained in his office. He allowed the depression to settle.

If this murder had never happened, Jack Cartland would have been content to amble on to his retirement, with his regret contained. Now, having seen a glimpse of hope, his desire to go out with a metaphorical crash of cymbals had become an obsession. He ate with it, slept with it—and was off his food and had no more than three hours sleep a night.

Which is why he was depressed. The case had sauntered to a stand-still. Although the story was no smaller in the national press, it had been moved to page two. Nothing was happening. There were no real developments. The excitement in Stilton was settling; some people were beginning to talk of other things.

Inspector Cartland clenched and unclenched his fists as he walked. His lumpy face was grim. He got no pleasure out of the glances of recognition thrown his way.

To himself he insisted, He had to find something, and it had to be on Harold Lunn, because Lunn had to be the one. There was his print in the house, his shaky alibi, and his rush to Mrs. Foster's after the first questioning, this possible redherring telephone call, his refusal of permission for a housesearch, even his non-possession of a coal-hammer. There was the tall man who parked his car and went toward Gorse Manor, for which Lunn held the only available key. He must be the one.

Cartland had become positive that Lunn had been in the house on the night of the murder. It was not a feeling, an intuition. It was there in the man's eyes and a twitch of the lips whenever that question came up. The question disturbed Lunn. He answered it with a special quality of vehemence.

If, the inspector thought, he could get enough evidence to go to trial, the rest would be easy. Under attack in the witness box, the keeper of the alibi, Mrs. Foster, would soon let the poor frail thing loose.

Next to physical evidence, the biggest lack was motive.

Jack Cartland had played with this, especially during the wakeful patches of night, when ugliness walks. There were many reasons for murder, and in this case most of them could be made to fit. Set aside was profit—Mrs. Lunn's financial state and expectations had been thoroughly checked.

While the sun shone, Cartland tended to the milder motives: sudden rage, despair, fear. In the cell of night, he favoured evil.

He knew, however, that murder is never a novel concept in the killer's nether mind. The man who, handling a gun, abruptly shoots his wife because of that one civilisation-piercing word or gesture has not at that moment become a murderer. He was that in childhood—as all people are—before began his conversion from a savage to an inchoate member of society. He retrogressed toward his destiny the day he met his wife; and continued to do so with every squabble.

Now, walking the bright streets, Cartland saw with an interior eye one of his variations on the same theme—Lunn and wife at home together.

She is taunting him with the fact of her latest lover. He, goaded beyond endurance, hits her with the first thing that comes to hand. She dies. Panicky, he takes the body to Gorse Manor and leaves it in the study, one hope being that death will be assumed due to supernatural causation.

The truth ran something like that, the inspector thought. It would all fall into place with one piece of evidence. Just one.

He turned a corner and was in Market Street. It was a narrow, snaking lane with outdoor stalls spotted along the sides. Saturdays the stalls were packed awning to awning and the roadway was covered by a slow-moving crowd.

In the gutters by the produce stands lay discarded, rotting fruit and vegetables. There was a smell like honey on sadness; a smell like nostalgia.

Cartland walked the length of the street, started back. He had seen only one hardware stall. Reaching it, he stopped and clasped his hands behind and looked over the array of goods.

There was a large selection of hammers, from sledge to ball-peen. Jack Cartland's eyes settled on a small implement with an oblong head.

"Just the job, they are."

He looked up. The speaker was short and fat. He wore a butcher's striped smock. A black bowler was tilted over his eyes.

The inspector said, "You've quite a choice."

"Claw, riveting, boilermaker, bricklayer, blacksmith, ball-peen, cross-peen, machinist, spalling, prospecting."

"Which kind was it the man bought? You know, the man you telephoned Mr. Harold Lunn about."

The dealer stared at him stupidly. Raising a slow hand, he pushed up his bowler. "Come again, mate?"

Cartland showed his card. "CID."

The stall-holder looked offended. "What you bothering me for?"

Jack Cartland explained, adding, "So I'd like a chat with the man who made the call."

"Wasn't me."

"Partner, assistant?"

"I'm on me own," the vendor said. He was intrigued now, leaning forward as if afraid of losing a single word. "It's that there murder, eh?"

Cartland nodded, looking at the hammers. Only the baby

sledge was a possibility. Its big relative would cave a skull in, the others all had curves or cuts.

"This little one," he said. "Sold many lately?"

"Two or three every week. People use 'em for coal. It was one like that, was it?"

"How many other ironmongery stalls are there here, on Saturdays?"

"Two. But they don't handle them hammers. They don't have anywhere near my selection."

"Look," Cartland said, "would you recognise, or do you know, anyone who bought one of these recently?"

The man shook his head sadly. "I don't look at their faces much. Only their money."

"Do you know Harold Lunn?"

"No."

Which seemed to end that, Cartland thought. The telephone call was either from yet another crank, or Lunn had invented it as a self-aid—one that was so feeble it could only have been sired by fear, mothered by desperation.

Leaving Market Street, the inspector told himself he was not being really thorough. The caller might have been a passer-by or another stall-holder.

He pushed the thought off.

After a lunch of beer and sandwiches, Jack Cartland went to the town hall for the inquest on Smith, the tramp. The fronting street was deserted, there were no constables on duty. In the council chamber, only fifteen people were present, six of them the jury.

Evidence took ten minutes. There was no mention of police negligence. The jury produced a verdict without leaving their seats: suicide while the balance of the mind was disturbed.

"They always say that," Jack Cartland grumbled, though satisfied with the result. He was walking out of the chamber with Dr. Patcher.

"It has a nice ring to it, Jack."

"I don't know why folk who kill themselves should always be considered crackers."

The doctor said, "It might have its uses, that verdict. Could be it puts a little brake on suicide."

"How?"

"Well, a proud person would have second thoughts about doing himself in if he knows he'll be called insane."

Cartland grunted. He said, "The law isn't always honest."

"No. Nor humane. But it's the only law we've got."

Outside, they strolled along to the doctor's car. Patcher asked, "How's the case going, Jack?"

The inspector told him; and sighed at how dull it sounded.

"So what's your next move?"

Cartland gave one of his big, quick shrugs. "Dunno. Maybe I'll take a run out to Gorse Manor. Poke about."

"Creepy bloody place."

"You reckon it's really haunted, Bert?"

The doctor shook his head. "I don't believe in ghosts."

"Nor I. A lot do, though. Lunn for one. And he's no fool."

"True."

"It's supposed to be the ghost of a little girl, I've heard."

"I thought it was her grandfather."

Cartland said, "She died of gangrene or something terrible like that. They brought in dozens of doctors."

"Double pneumonia. Three doctors. My father was one of 'em."

"That right?" Cartland said, looking at his wristwatch.

"Poor dad. He wanted to go in for surgery but his sight began to fail."

"Did you know the other doctors?"

"Before my time. One got killed in a car accident. The other was struck off for doing abortions."

"Serve him right."

The doctor slid a forefinger up his nose to settle his spectacles. "Oh, I don't know. The law isn't always honest or humane, is it, Jack?"

Cartland looked at him in surprise. Dr. Patcher winked. "Give you a lift to the station?"

Fifteen minutes later, Jack Cartland drew a police car to a stop on the gravel before Gorse Manor. With the key he had taken from Harold Lunn, he let himself into the house. Its silence made him uncomfortable. He put down his feet weightily as he went from room to room and then up the staircase and along the gallery.

He stood in the study doorway. Reluctantly, he allowed his gaze to come to rest on the mantelshelf. After a moment he imagined:

She's standing on that wing-chair. She's looking at the ceiling to see where she can fix some trick to pull on her husband. She overbalances. She hurtles off the chair and crashes into the mantelshelf.

Fair.

She's downstairs. She either sees Smith or is chased by him. Runs up and in here. She trips and falls against the mantel. Or the same trip and fall if playing a game with lover or husband.

Fair. And you couldn't blame the man involved for keeping quiet about it.

Jack Cartland realised that he had come here for this reason only. He swung grumpily away, went downstairs, and left the house.

Back at the police station, he found Detective Tarkinson waiting in his office. Glumly he said:

"Woman called twice, sir. Wants to talk to you."

"Name?"

The detective shook his head. "Could be another crank. Except she didn't sound like one."

Inspector Cartland sat heavily in his chair. "I'm getting tired of these stupid calls. We've never had so many on a case."

"This one's caused quite a stir."

Cartland asked, "Want a job?"

"Eager and willing."

"Check the stalls on either side of and across from the hardware merchant. You know what to ask about."

"No score this morning?"

"Blanks all over the bloody place."

Tarkinson left.

The inspector sat on at his desk. For something to do he opened the bundle of possessions willed to him by the dead tramp. They told him nothing. He sent for a constable to take them out to the incinerator.

At five o'clock the telephone rang. The caller, who had a high, breathless-sounding voice, wanted to know if Mr. Cartland was back yet.

"Inspector Cartland speaking."

"Well, I'd like to tell you about a dream I had."

Go and drown yourself. Don't you know it's illegal to waste the time of the police? See a doctor. Get off the line, you blithering idiot.

These phrases Jack Cartland tasted with affectionate relish, before saying, "Yes, ma'am. Go on."

"It was today. After lunch. I always take a nap. It does you good, I always say."

"And the dream?"

"It was in the grounds of Gorse Manor. In the trees near the back of the gatehouse. I saw a man digging. He was digging something up and looking around as if scared of being seen. You know what I mean."

"Yes," the inspector said. He stifled a yawn.

"That's all there is to it except I knew, the way you do in dreams, that it was twelve noon and tomorrow. I thought I'd better tell you about it."

"I see, Mrs. Foster."

"What?"

"You are Mrs. Foster, aren't you?"

"No. I don't want to give you my name. But the thing is, I

am quite a bit psychic. I've had dreams before that've come true. Honestly."

"Fine. Thank you for calling, ma'am."

"My pleasure. I hope it helps."

"Good afternoon."

Cartland smiled as he put down the receiver. You certainly got some odd ones, he thought.

He went home at six, after hearing Tarkinson's report from the market—negative. He stodged through a meal of beans on toast, washed, and went out to his local pub, where he drank seven pints of beer, ignored all attempts to be drawn on the Lunn case, played darts, and argued about the scoring.

His sleep was deep and dreamless, which is what he had hoped for and was the reason for his drinking beyond his usual intake.

He was in his office at nine, and annoyed to find himself thinking about that last anonymous telephone call. Twelve noon in the trees behind the gatehouse.

"Ridiculous!" he said aloud.

And he went on thinking about it.

Only once during the morning was he side-tracked. Detective Keller came in, newly returned from a visit to the home town of Mrs. Rosalind Lunn. He had uncovered no old boy friends, no relatives, no item of interest.

At eleven-thirty, quietly furious with himself, Jack Cartland took Keller and Constable Pierce out to a car. He explained as he drove. Into the silence that followed he snapped:

"All right. I know it's bloody stupid. But it's better than sitting on my backside waiting for something to happen."

"Yes, sir," the two men said in unison.

The constable added, "As a matter of fact, sir, these things have sometimes come off. I've read about it."

"That right, Pierce?"

"Yes, sir."

"Good," Cartland said. He silently blessed the young man and felt less furious.

Passing through the gates of Gorse Manor, he drove on and parked the car out of sight behind the house. He and the other two walked back.

"To do this properly," Jack Cartland said, "we should surround the area. But for one thing that might block the suspect's approach, for another—well, we're not really expecting anyone."

At the gatehouse he knocked and told the caretaker they were going to wait at the rear for someone, and asked would she stay inside and keep quiet.

She nodded.

They went behind the small building. There were rubbish bins, empty rabbit hutches, a kennel in which logs were stacked, a gardening shed which a plank buttress was keeping upright if not erect.

Facing these, starting from six feet away, were the trees, youngsters with boles as thick as lamp-posts.

The constable crouched behind a dustbin, Cartland and Keller stood behind the leaning shed.

The detective asked, "Are we going to Mrs. Lunn's funeral tomorrow?"

The inspector was looking at his watch. It showed ten minutes to twelve. He said, "Shh."

They waited. The seconds ticked by. Jack Cartland was surprised to realise he was growing tense. He didn't like that. He felt sure he was in for a disappointment. The whole idea, in fact, was absurd.

He was tempted to call off the non-ambush. His feelings dissuaded him. Forgetting the possibility of disappointment, he allowed the tension to grow.

He twitched nervously when the constable hissed. He shot a look to where the young man crouched. Pierce was pointing. Jack Cartland sidled to the corner of his cover and looked in the indicated direction.

A figure was moving through the trees.

It was merely a dark shape which sliced in and out of view between middle-distant trunks. There was no accompanying sound, none of the rustle a person would make were he moving casually.

Cartland looked at his watch. It told twelve o'clock. When he looked up again, the figure had stopped. Next, it sank low. Next came the faint sound of scraping.

Cartland's tension was strong. He could feel his heart nattering at his top ribs.

He glanced at Keller, signalled to the constable, and began to move forward. He kept a cautious eye on the ground underfoot, wary of dry leaves and sticks.

Pierce was abreast of him on the left, Keller on his right. Both men were tight-faced, unblinking, like gamblers awaiting the turn of a card.

The person ahead was now several yards away. The sound of scraping was louder. Cartland could see slices of a bent back, the sole of a shoe.

Detective Keller stepped on a twig.

The crack it made was as loud as a shot from a .32 rifle. Keller and the constable and Jack Cartland, they froze.

Oddly, the scraping and the gentle movement of the bent shoulders went on without pause.

After exchanging glances, the three men moved forward, the juniors following Cartland's lead by continuing stealth. With two yards to go, the inspector signalled his men to stop. He went on alone.

A clearing opened up. At its edge, Cartland halted. He folded his arms, nodded, and said mildly, "Hello, Mr. Shield."

The young man started, looked around. He stared with worried eyes. A flush spread across his smooth, juvenile cheeks.

"Oh," he said.

At his knees was a hole, a foot across and some six inches

deep. He had been scraping at it with a flat stone. Drooping, lowering his eyes, he tossed the stone aside tiredly

Jack Cartland turned his head to say, "Pierce. Bring the car along, please."

He went closer to Michael Shield. Looking down into the hole, he saw a smooth piece of wood protruding from the loose soil. He squatted and lifted the wood. It was a hammer.

He brought it close to his face, peering at the head and the handle. Brushing the implement free of soil, he put it in his pocket as he rose.

"Come along, lad," he said.

Michael Shield got up. Cartland took his arm and they went back through the trees together, Detective Keller following.

The car was drawing up. Cartland and the young man got in the back. Not a word was spoken until they stopped outside the police station.

Cartland said to the men in front, "You two go and get yourselves a cup of tea. And don't talk this up."

He took Michael Shield inside the building via the side door and along to his office. He closed the door.

"Sit down, son."

Shield sat. Cartland went around to his own chair and put the hammer on the desk.

"Now," he said. He leaned forward and interlaced the tips of his fingers. "Now, young man, what've you got to say for yourself?"

Shield sat limply, hands on his lap. His head was down, his gaze on the front of the desk.

Jack Cartland asked, "When did you buy this hammer?"

No answer.

"Never mind. I'll tell you. You bought it since the inquest on Mrs. Lunn."

Michael Shield frowned.

Cartland said, "*Where* you bought it doesn't matter. You bought it because it fitted the description. Right?"

The young man looked up. He appeared to be worriedly puzzled.

The inspector asked, "Do you want to tell me, son, or shall I tell you?"

Michael Shield, after clearing his throat, said faintly, "I don't understand."

"Okay. If that's the way you want it. Now. You bought this hammer and then telephoned me, pretending to be some woman who considers herself to be psychic. I thought at the time there was something a bit odd about that voice. You gave me this story about a dream, and went along there today to make it come true. You began to dig and pretended not to hear when we made a bloody great noise in closing in." He shook his head. "You just haven't done very well at all."

Unclasping his hands, Cartland pointed at the hammer.

"The impression you hoped to give was that you were digging it up, getting it from where you'd hidden it. In fact, you scraped a hole and put the hammer *in*. It's dry, son. If it had been there for any length of time the handle would be damp and the head would be tinged with rust."

Cartland saw there was sweat on the young man's brow. His face was pale and unsteady, a slight tremble in the cheeks and lips.

"Mr. Shield," the inspector asked, "would you like to tell me why you did this?"

No answer.

"No? All right. I'll do the talking. You did it for one of two reasons, and perhaps a combination of the two. The first is to draw suspicion away from your friend, Harold Lunn. You felt nice and safe because of the knowledge that we couldn't, when it came down to hard evidence, connect you with the murder."

The inspector added, "Come to think of it, Lunn himself might have put you up to this game."

The young man's eyes flickered—and Cartland saw he had scored a miss on that one. Otherwise, he knew he was right.

He went on, "Secondly, you did it to bring on to yourself some of the sick glamour of this murder case, as a hundred-odd other people have tried to do in one way or another. You were looking for drama."

Michael Shield was watching him closely. He whispered, "Is that what you think?"

The inspector nodded. *"He tends to dramatise.* Dr. Klein told me that about you."

There was a palpable change in the atmosphere. The young man's watchfulness had become a stare.

Cartland nodded again, a long slow nod to convince. "That's right—Dr. Klein. After you gave me details about your background, I checked. Naturally. It's part of my job. You understand?"

A nod.

"I was able to contact the doctor by telephone. He was interested to know how you were getting along. I told him you seemed fine and I explained the situation. He said there was no harm in you whatever. A fondness for drama is common enough. He said that if I'd ever suspected you for a moment of being involved with murder, forget it. It's against your nature to hurt anyone. Entirely against your nature."

Jack Cartland smiled sympathetically. "So there we are, lad. You've accomplished nothing with your little game. Except waste some of our time."

Michael Shield looked down. The sweat on his brow formed into rivulets.

Cartland got up to circle the desk. "From now on, I hope you're going to behave yourself. In fact, if there's nothing to hold you in Stilton, you might as well leave. There's nothing you can do for Harold Lunn."

With a tired motion, the young man pulled a handkerchief from his pocket and raised it to his brow. Out with the handkerchief came a key, which fell glitteringly to the floor. Shield stared down at the shiny object.

Sighing, Jack Cartland stooped and retrieved the key. He

slipped it back in the young man's pocket. In with it he put
the hammer, saying:

"Pull yourself together, lad. You're not being a help to anyone, you know. Come on."

Mopping at his brow, Michael Shield got up and moved to
the door, which Cartland drew open.

"Off you go, son. And stay out of trouble. Meaning, no
more nonsense."

He closed the door after Shield and returned slowly to the
desk, shaking his head.

———◆▶———

They went past the last house of the last suburb. On either
side of the road were thorn hedges, dense and high. Over
them leaned trees.

Jack Cartland switched off the headlights. Although the
still-burning side-lights would not normally have given
sufficient illumination, they were enough now; in fact, the
light from the moon was stronger. It made the road a band of
silver-white crossed with the trees' deep black shadows.

As each of these bands of black passed over the car—flick,
flick, flick—Michael Shield blinked. It was like a blink anyway, the flash of dark.

Now that the headlights were off, the area was familiar to
Michael. This is the way it had been a week ago, though not
quite so brightly lit, and he had no fear now, was not alone
and had no awfulness waiting for him.

Michael felt strong.

He turned with a smile to the woman at his side. "How are
you feeling, Mrs. Foster?"

"Fine, thank you. Just fine."

"Good."

"I'm so glad, Mr. Shield, that you agree to this."

"I was happy to, ma'am. I'm glad I was asked."

A pleasant boy, Mrs. Foster thought again. There weren't

many like that any more. You'd think good manners had gone out of fashion, or were silly or something. It was all the violence in the world and in comic books. Youngsters thought it was smart to be tough.

With an agitated movement of her back, Mrs. Foster recalled the visit to her cottage of the two young detectives.

They had been offensive, crude. Anyone would have thought she was a criminal the way they snapped questions at her. Of course, it was true that she was fibbing about the time of Mr. Lunn's arrival that night, but they couldn't possibly know that and so had no right to accuse her of it. They wouldn't have acted that way if Mr. Cartland had been there. He was a gentleman.

Mrs. Foster played a look of affection over the inspector. She felt like reaching out to touch his back. Mrs. Foster always wanted to touch people she sensed were simpatico.

But those two detectives, she thought. They were the limit. They'd turned her inside out like an old sock, asked so many questions that she didn't know if she was coming or going. Finally, the one with hair like red bubbles had said, "Look, we know Lunn killed his wife. You've either got to be lying or mistaken." It was then she gathered the courage to ask them to leave.

Mrs. Foster closed her eyes while she shook her head. It had been awful, she mused. But there had been other times like that during the week. A terrible week altogether. Terrible.

———◆———

How dreadful it all is, she thought. Poor Mr. Lunn standing there so pale, so ill-looking, his eyes staring into the grave, his body as limp as anything, as if he hadn't a pennyworth of strength left, and the parson muttering away there like an auctioneer, and those people with Mr. Lunn, relations they must be, they couldn't care less, that woman with the silly hat was glaring at the other woman's coat as if she'd like to set it on fire.

Mrs. Foster turned her attention away from the immediate area of the graveside.

Just look at those reporters over there, talking among themselves and smoking. Cheeky lot. It had been such a pleasure when they'd called at the cottage to send them off with a flea in their ear. Cheeky devils.

Returning her attention to those around her, Mrs. Foster thought: Inspector Cartland, nice man he is, at least he's got the decency to stand quiet-like and pay heed to the parson, and so has that young man with the baby face, who's really sad you can tell, he could be the lodger that used to live with them. That made three decent folk here. That horrible crowd at the church, and here at the cemetery gate. They should be locked up. If I had my way . . .

The minister closed his book.

Mr. Lunn stepped forward, picked up a handful of earth and threw it onto the coffin. One by one, the others present performed the same rite. Mrs. Foster was last.

Turning from the grave, she looked around for Mr. Lunn. She wanted to say the customary words of condolence. They had been said already, but the mores of burial required their repetition to round out the ceremony.

Mr. Lunn was occupied. He and Inspector Cartland were talking together. They were being eyed with interest by the newspaper reporters.

Mrs. Foster decided to forget protocol. The air was chill, the sky was darkening with the first frowns of evening, her stomach and soul craved the comfort of a cup of tea.

She walked on, passed haughtily the gaping people at the graveyard gate, and headed for home.

Half an hour later, tea drunk, Mrs. Foster slipped into a doze in her chair by the fire. She was aroused by a knock on the front door.

The room was dark. Switching on the light, Mrs. Foster

mused that her caller was sure to be one of the neighbours, wanting to know about the funeral, with hopes of some dramatic happening.

She pulled a face. The neighbours had been a nuisance throughout the past days. She hadn't made herself popular by her refusal to gossip.

Mrs. Foster opened the front door. The visitor was Mr. Lunn. Fussing over him like a nanny over a returned runaway, she brought him inside, sat him beside the fire, and gave him a glass of sherry.

She took the chair opposite. "You do look tired, Mr. Lunn."

"I am. I need a week's sleep."

"Now that it's all over, you should go away for a nice holiday."

He shook his head. "It isn't all over. Not yet."

"How's that?"

"I'm still a suspect."

"Ridiculous," she snorted. "The silliest thing I ever heard in my life."

"Do you know where I've been tonight, Mrs. Foster?"

"The police station, I suppose."

"To begin with, yes. Then Cartland and I and five other men drove to the edge of town. The other men were constables in plain clothes. They were similar to me in build."

Mrs. Foster blinked. "What was it all about?"

"As you know," Mr. Lunn said, "the night my wife was killed I followed her. Part of the way by car, the rest on foot. A woman saw me park the car and walk on. Or anyway, I'm assuming it was me."

He smiled grimly. "Tonight was a sort of identity parade."

"Oh. I see."

"I and the other men, we each took a turn at walking past the woman's house. She watched from a window."

Mrs. Foster leaned forward tensely. "Well?"

Mr. Lunn spread his hands. "Here I am, still free. I imagine the woman couldn't make a positive identification. Cartland said nothing."

Mrs. Foster relaxed with a sigh. "Thank God for that."

"Yes, I suppose I should be thankful for small mercies. But I can't be. I can't look at it that way. I'm surrounded by professional and private suspicion, and it's pushing me to the wall."

"Poor Mr. Lunn," she said unhappily. "If only there was something we could do."

He nodded briskly, for the first time showing animation. He said, "That's it."

"Mmm?"

He got up and began to pace. "It same to me when I left the police. It's a good idea. You might not agree. You might think I'm crazy or clutching at straws. But really, I've come to the point where I don't care what anyone thinks."

Like a tennis spectator in slow motion, she was watching her visitor as he moved. She said:

"That's understandable, Mr. Lunn."

"Somehow I've got to end this suspicion. The police have nothing definite. How could they have, since I'm innocent? It was either that tramp or a lover of Rosalind's."

"Yes."

"Frankly, I don't much care if the killer's ever found. Not as far as justice is concerned. What I want is for me to be absolutely cleared."

"So what's your idea, Mr. Lunn?"

He came and stood over her like a protagonist, his arms folded tightly. His eyes were keen.

"What if we hold a seance?" he said. "You and I and Inspector Cartland. We hold it in the upstairs study of Gorse Manor on the night of the full moon. The three of us there around the Ouija board."

Mrs. Foster nodded slowly. She licked her lips. "I see."

"This time it will be in absolute earnest. You could even say it would be a matter of life or death."

"Yes, but why there, Mr. Lunn? And why the full moon?"

"It's then that the place is said to be at its most powerful in supernatural terms. That might help with Rosalind."

He leaned down. "Mrs. Foster, it's my wife we'll be trying to contact."

"I understand. That's the reason for the place."

"Quite. She died there. Less than a week ago. With the study's occult influences, and with your spiritual gifts, she may be able to get through to us. All the circumstances will be favourable. You see?"

"Yes."

He returned to his chair, drank off the sherry at a gulp, and leaned forward.

"What do you think of the idea? Sound or silly?"

"Sound," she said, and now began to feel the first itch of excitement.

This, she thought, could be it. *It.* This could be the moment she had been waiting for, it seemed all her days, and was beginning to think would never come, what with growing older and everything. All the influences being right, she would finally and conclusively *know.* It could be the most important night of her life.

"Sound," Mrs. Foster said again, smiling.

He returned the smile. It was good to see it.

She asked, "Will Mr. Cartland agree?"

"I'm sure he will. I'll convince him. Oh yes, he'll come with us all right."

They were silent for a moment.

Thoughtfully, Mrs. Foster said, "I didn't know your wife. Neither did Mr. Cartland. Might it not be a good thing, help the influences, if we got someone else besides you? Someone who knew Mrs. Lunn real well. One of her family perhaps."

"Well, there is no family. And she had no close friends."

"The young man who was staying with you."

Mr. Lunn puckered his mouth in that way of his which brought out white spots on the skin.

"There's a thought for you," he said. "They were quite close. Shield knew her, possibly, in a way I never did. They talked a lot. And"—pointing—"he saw her an hour or so before she died."

"There you are."

"Yes, it's a thought all right."

"If he'll help."

"He said he'd do anything he could. But the only problem is, he's afraid of ghosts. He said as much one time when I was talking about Gorse Manor."

"All the better, Mr. Lunn. He's a believer. He'll take it seriously. He'll really concentrate."

"If we can get him there," he said. He looked at his watch and rose. "We'll soon find out."

———————◆—————————

On the right appeared a wall. It was three feet tall and topped with rails whose heads owned vicious-looking spikes.

The long stretch of brickwork threw back the sound of the police car as it passed—a hollow hissing sound like someone endlessly exhaling.

Glancing at the rails with their tops like halberds, Inspector Jack Cartland winced. Mrs. Foster was reminded of a platoon of invisible pikemen. Harold Lunn, he looked right through the rails at the trees and thought of the old dark house waiting beyond, and of what might be waiting inside.

Michael Shield saw nothing. He was musing on the last exchange between himself and the medium at his side. She had said she was glad he had agreed to come along tonight. His answer had been that he was glad he had been asked.

Glad? he thought. The wrong word. Too weak. But, of course, quite right for the circumstances. Being asked was a stroke of luck.

Michael put his arms across his chest; not folded there; placed one above the other.

The police car rounded a bend in the road. Ahead stood the gatehouse. One window showed a glimmer of light. Opposite, the guardian griffin squatted on its pillar.

Inspector Cartland cleared his throat gently. He felt somehow that this was a necessary prelude to speech, that sudden words would startle his passengers.

"I'll just stop here a minute," he said. "If nobody minds."

Harold Lunn looked around. "What for?"

"So the caretaker won't call the station and complain of someone being at the house." He added a tart, "Obviously."

Passing through the gate, he brought the car to a halt on the driveway. He got out and walked back.

Michael Shield leaned forward. He stared at the broad lane of gravel. He had never before paused to look at it from this angle. A spot in his memory was scraped, activated.

Michael blinked slowly.

———◆———

"I can't help it," he said. His voice was dull, the words were droning from his slack mouth.

He looked up from his limp sprawl in an armchair. "I know it's bad. And I hate myself. But I go on doing it."

Michael was not, to his continuing surprise, in a police station. Around him in the small room were all the neat pieces found in the front parlour of a private house.

He dimly recalled his walk here from the park. His eyes had been blurred with tears, the remains of that sobbing of defeat when, in turning away from the screaming woman, he had been grabbed by the man. He recalled being hurried off, being ushered into this room, being brought a cup of tea by a woman with a worried face, being rejoined by the man.

"I've been doing it for years," Michael said now. There was a small release in his being able to say it.

The man stood before him in the centre of the room, hands

attackingly on hips. He asked, in a tone which didn't match the stance:

"Do you know why you do it?"

"No."

"But you like it."

"It disgusts me."

"You haven't touched your tea."

Michael shook his head. "Sorry."

"Tell me your name, please."

"Michael Shield." He added his address.

"It's surprising you've never been caught," the man said. He was large-framed and heavy, his green pullover stretched so tight it showed the white shirt underneath. He wore an athlete's training pants. His round, ruddy face was topped by premature baldness.

He said, "Some of the women you insulted. They must have gone to the police. That woman of today might be reporting the incident at this very moment. Did you never think about that?"

Michael moved his hands. "I don't know. It didn't matter. I had to do it." He had no fear. He merely felt drained.

The man studied him for a moment. He asked, "Do you remember me telling you I'm a doctor?"

"No."

"Charles White. MD. GP. The surgery's next door."

"I see."

"I'm breaking the law by not turning you over to the police. My wife thinks I'm mad."

"It's good of you. I—"

"No," the doctor said. "Sensible or stupid. I don't know which. This is foreign ground to me. If I'm being good, it's to women who may be future victims of this awful thing."

Michael watched him and waited.

After a pause, Dr. White said, "Tell me about yourself."

"Well, what?"

"Anything. Everything. Just talk."

Michael talked.

An hour later they left the house and drove in the doctor's car to Michael's home. Inside, Dr. White looked around and said:

"The reason I came here was to see if you were telling the truth. At least partly. Sit down, Michael. I'll tell you my proposal."

Puzzled through his weariness, Michael sat.

Standing nearby in his stance of attack, the doctor said, "You're a sick boy, you know. In what way especially, I have no idea. But it's obvious that something has to be done. Agreed?"

"I don't know."

"Prison, it seems to me, is not the answer. It never cured anyone of anything. But you shouldn't be allowed to roam around and do this thing to women. So, Michael, unless you accept my proposal, I shall be forced to take the matter to the police."

"Oh."

"I'll even bear witness against you."

Unblinking, Michael watched the doctor. "Go on, please."

"There's a hospital not far from here," Dr. White said. A frown came and went as he added, "It's for people with nervous disorders."

Michael sat a fraction straighter. The doctor said, nodding, "All right, it's a mental institution. Call it a nut house. Call it anything you like. They treat everyone from the neurotic to the insane."

Sagging, Michael closed his eyes. He opened them again when the doctor went on in a more cheerful voice:

"The staff's a good crowd and the physicians are excellent, first-rate. The place is state-run, of course, so treatment is free for—"

"Dr. White," Michael said flatly. "What's your proposal?"

"Isn't it obvious?"

"No," Michael lied.

The doctor said, "I want you to go in as a voluntary patient." He hurried on, "I'll make all the arrangements. I'll smooth the way. The only thing you need do is go there and sign the necessary papers. I'll even take you myself. I know the people. There'll be no problems. And listen. Listen, Michael."

"Yes?"

"This could be the best thing that ever happened to you."

Michael looked down. His reaction to the proposal was dulled by weariness. He cared little about either of the offered directions, except that one seemed less involved than the other.

"In a few months or even weeks, Michael, you could be out again. And well. And happy."

Michael said nothing.

Dr. White asked, "Are you happy with the way things are?"

Michael shook his head slowly. "No."

"Then give it a try. In fact, you'll have to. Otherwise . . ."

"Yes. I know."

The doctor bent down, hands on knees. "What do you say?"

Two days later, Michael entered Broadhaven Hospital.

He stayed for three years.

It was the most intolerable period of his life. He had a room of his own, he was treated well, he wore his own clothes, he was allowed to roam wherever he chose; but for Michael the hospital was a quiet hell.

Two factors sustained him during these years of an existence which, at best, was dull and pointless. One was Dr. Klein.

A young man, not yet thirty, the psychiatrist had recently come to England from Germany. He was small and thin and intense, with piercing black eyes as disturbing at times as those of some of the inmates. He wore a pointed beard which seemed somehow right because of his broken accent.

Dr. Klein was not popular with all his colleagues. A hospital being as prone to gossip as any village or prison, it was common knowledge among the patients that the German had the reputation of being difficult and revolutionary. He did not, for instance, have any faith in electric shock treatment, which everyone knew to be marvellous—except those patients on whom it was used. In some ways he went backwards, was old-fashioned. He talked of the value of hypnotism. Behind his back, the other doctors called him Anton Mesmer.

Michael was afraid of Dr. Klein; and looked forward to their weekly sessions of talk. Sitting semi-prone in a reclining chair, Michael answered questions at rambling length. He held nothing back. Never had he been so outgoing. It was due to a combination of release for his withdrawn state the rest of the time, and worry that Dr. Klein might lose interest in him if he hesitated. Sometimes he even lied to add flavour to stories which, to himself, sounded boring.

Except for one secret, Michael told everything he could remember. But it was the earlier times, Michael's childhood, that the doctor seemed to find particularly interesting.

Apart from their two-hour sessions every week, Michael saw Dr. Klein only when he felt the desire to swear in front of a woman. These occasions were rare. The female inmates with whom he came in contact were odd and apathetic creatures, to say the least, who looked incapable of either anger or joy; the nurses saw disgusting behaviour every day. Michael told himself it was the clinical atmosphere that held down his unfortunate predilection, and was thankful. When he did get an inkling of that old sensation which spelled an imminent foray, he would hurriedly seek out his doctor, talk, and win the fight.

Life at Broadhaven was a routine of sleep, eat, handicrafts, eat, walks and radio and socialising, eat, sleep. Michael considered himself lucky when he landed the job of raking leaves off the gravel drive which led to the locked and guarded gates. It was a non-life. Everyone was solicitous and decent, and Michael was unhappy.

After a time, when his memory had been scoured and emptied of past events, Michael did less talking during sessions in the reclining chair. Dr. Klein performed monologues, interrupting himself occasionally to ask a question.

What he said was nonsense, as far as Michael was concerned, which made him less dependent on the doctor and less satisfied with his existence. Some of Dr. Klein's statements were unintelligible, the rest unacceptable.

According to him, Michael was a spiritual masochist. Though he shrank from the physical, he craved the abstract forms of subjugation. The satisfaction he thus derived was in reference to his constant need for control, authority, which meant security.

Nonsense, Michael thought. He began, deliberately, to miss out on some of his visits to the doctor's office, claiming various forms of indisposition.

The routine of institutional living went on. One month was like another, one year the same as that just past.

Yet Michael did have his second sustaining factor, that one secret he had withheld from Dr. Klein. It was his daydream. Previously, he had played with it, like a kitten with a ball. Now he was like a cat with a mouse; there was gravity behind the play.

It was a marvellous help, the fantasy. He would live it sometimes quickly, a glutton, using up all its wonderful scenes and ramifications in the space of a single hour. Generally, however, he would go over it with slow, lingering care, making it last for three or four days. Resting, doing handicrafts, scraping leaves, he would be lost to the outside world.

Interruptions he resented. But they were vaguely enjoyable too. His secret was waiting. No one could touch it. No one knew of it. He escaped into it from the hospital whenever he wanted, and never once did he see it as monstrous. To him it was lovely, and noble.

Michael's daydream was quite straightforward. He wanted to be hanged by the neck until dead.

Not at any time did he allow the projector of his imagination to show the last scene. Nor did he ever permit the first. It was that long, complex act between which mattered, which thrilled and gave comfort.

Everybody has a fantasy life. No one is without imagination. Even the dullard will have brief visions of himself winning, say, a dart match. At the other end, the piteous end of the scale, the total schizoid is so immersed in his dream that he thinks he is imagining reality.

All fantasies give satisfaction. Nobody ever dreamed himself sad, except enjoyably so.

Michael would tremble with pleasure whenever he slipped away from the now. His face would slacken to repose, his eyes would dull to blankness. He was seeing the ultimate of his desire.

The idea had come from a detective novel he had read at the age of seventeen; had read three times. Soon thereafter the daydream had made its first appearance. Rough, ill-scripted, it flickered through his mind like a 1910 two-reeler. Repetition gave it length and refinement. In Broadhaven Hospital, the years and his increased need had brought the fantasy to a fine sophistication.

He is running away. It is night and he is afraid. The garden he is crossing has large, leafless trees which seem to grasp at him as he passes underneath. He runs swiftly. He must escape. Behind him in the hunting lodge is a dead person, shot through the heart. He has killed his enemy and must get away before the alarm is . . .

Lights! Shouts! The barking of dogs!

He puts on speed.

And reaches the wall. He had forgotten about the wall. It is high and topped with barbed wire. He cannot go back. The baying of the dogs is louder, harsh voices are calling, flashlights sweep over the garden. He leaps up. His hands get nowhere near the top. He is small.

Turning, he runs along beside the brickwork. His lungs are heaving. The thick grass pulls at his legs and slows him down. He searches frantically for footholds in the wall. He sees none. The dogs are closing in. He glances back and sees the large, slavering mouths.

A tree appears. It is leaning toward the wall. He clasps the trunk and begins to haul himself up. The dogs snap at his shoes. Higher and higher he climbs, until the barbed wire is close. He steps onto it, then drops over the other side onto soft earth.

Gasping, he runs through narrow streets. They are dark. He is surrounded by blackness. When almost home, he sees someone he knows, an old woman who sells newspapers. She waves and calls his name. He looks away and runs on.

Home is an attic, one large room. The ceiling slopes, there is a tall window that looks out onto rooftops and chimneys. He flings himself onto the couch and sleeps, only to be awakened at dawn's first light by a pounding on the door.

There are three of them. They are huge men and wear dark uniforms. Their faces have a brutal grimness, their voices grate, their mere presence is an offence. They snarl questions while striding around the room and touching his cherished possessions.

He was home all night, he says. He often fell asleep with his clothes on. The mud on his shoes is from the park. He knew the dead person only slightly. They liked each other. He is stricken to hear of what has happened.

The tough policemen leave. Later, he goes out for breakfast. He realises he is being followed. Panicking, he runs. He is cornered down an alley and taken to police headquarters.

The three men are waiting. As before, they don't touch him. They sit him in a chair and shine lights in his face and shout at him and flay him with questions.

It goes on all day. There is nothing he can do to resist; they are so big, he is so small. He gets no respite. Although he continues to protest his innocence, the net draws tighter.

Someone has been found who heard him arguing with the dead person. He was seen outdoors, running, by the old woman who sells newspapers. He is known to own a gun. The soil on his shoes is the same as that of the hunting-lodge garden.

Finally, he breaks down. He confesses. He makes and signs a statement. The three policemen look at him with distaste. When they take him to a cell, they avoid body contact.

The days pass. Food is shoved at him through the bars. The warders are contemptuous, the other prisoners treat him like an outcast. He is a vile murderer. Scum. The lawyer who consents to take his brief hovers between indifference and disdain. The newspapers call him despicable, a crude killer, while extolling the virtues of the dead person.

The trial. The courtroom is an arena of staring people, eyes of hate. He is alone and small in the dock. Lawyers snap, the judge frowns, jurymen pull mouths of scorn. The verdict is guilty. Everyone breathes a sigh of satisfaction. The judge covers his wig with the black cap. He intones:

"Michael Shield, the jury has found you guilty of wilful murder and the sentence of the court upon you is that you be taken from this place to a lawful prison, and thence to a place of execution, and there you suffer death by hanging, and that your body be buried within the precincts of the prison in which you shall have been last confined before your execution, and may the Lord have mercy on your soul."

The death cell. For three weeks he is never alone night or day. Always there are two warders in attendance. They offer him no comfort. They despise him for what he is, resent him for causing them this drab duty. It is three weeks of muttered and unspoken abuse, of visits by a reproachful priest, of sleepless nights with the light ever burning, of wretched food and the pretence at card games and the constant watchfulness to prevent suicide and a growing, terrible tension.

The last meal. The last night. The early morning is slag-grey when he hears the sound he has been straining for and dreading: a jumble of soft, slow footsteps. They approach. His guards get up. He also stands. He is trembling. The door opens and in come the prison warden, the priest, the hang-man, and his assistant. They pause and look at him.

Michael never got further than that point, the entry. The scene would fade, and he would find himself dazedly back in an alien world.

But not for long. Soon he would again be running away from that hunting lodge, and from a victim who was always faceless and sexless.

Time had embellished the dream with many details, mainly on legal procedure. Some he had picked up in pre-hospital days, from books and newspapers. Some he had gathered in talk with inmates who had been in courtrooms and prisons. Some he got from the Broadhaven library. No researching scholar was more delighted than Michael when he came across an item he could use, such as the fact that the black cap of a sentencing judge was not a cap at all but a foot-square piece of cloth.

The fantasy was important to Michael's peace of mind, his stability. Yet as the years passed, even that dark tunnel of es-cape failed to keep him from finding the daily routine intoler-able. Furthermore, he knew he could never bring his dream to fruition. He was a cat with a toy mouse.

One day, complaining of Broadhaven on a rare visit to Dr. Klein, he was surprised to hear:

"Then why do you not leave, Mr. Shield?"

"Leave?"

Smiling, the doctor stroked his beard. "How long is it since you had the urge to abuse women?"

Michael shrugged off the question. It was unimportant. He couldn't remember the last time he had wanted to do that strange thing.

Dr. Klein asked, "Was it when you began missing our sessions here?"

"I can't remember."

"No matter. The desire has gone, I think. You should leave here."

"Tell me how."

The doctor spread his hands. "You are a voluntary patient. You could have left at any time. You may do so now. This afternoon."

Some days passed before Michael found the courage to go. Anxious and feeling odd, he walked to the railway station and got on the first train out. It was going to Stilton.

He stayed in a hotel for a time, answered an advertisement in the paper, and took lodgings. He lived with Mr. and Mrs. Lunn.

Within five months, Michael and Rosalind Lunn were lovers. The sex was pleasurable but Michael was not happy with the situation. Not until the night the impossible happened. Rosalind showed him the way to make his dream come true. When she had gone, he cried.

Throughout the following weeks of planning, Michael was consumed by a single question: Would he be capable of accepting this gift?

Mostly, he doubted it. He had never been able to bring himself to destroy anything animate. The sight of a dead bird made his heart ache. But there were times during those weeks when he was convinced that at the moment of truth he would have the courage, would be able to summon it for at least the duration of the needed three or four seconds. The question lived.

It lived until the rehearsal at Gorse Manor, a trial run of the killing of Harold Lunn. Michael survived his fear of the dark in the grounds, survived his terror in the hall—even when seeing a figure there—and prepared himself for the horror.

Up in the study, he and Rosalind talked for a while. Then

Michael stared into the alcove. He went on staring despite Rosalind's questions. Her voice became less querulous, more a nervous whisper.·

At last Michael spoke. He said:

"There is something behind you."

Convulsively, Rosalind clasped her hands together. "Stop it," she said weakly. "You're frightening me."

Michael moved out from behind the chair. He stepped closer to Rosalind, closer to the horror. He was shaking all over. He felt sure he couldn't go on.

His voice a hiss, his eyes still staring into the alcove, he said, "In the corner."

"No. Stop. Please. What is it?"

"Look."

"No."

Michael moved another step closer to Rosalind. He was within touching distance.

"Look behind you," he said.

She swung her head partway to the side. "No," she whispered. "Let's go. I want to go."

Now! thought Michael. The thought was a scream.

He gasped, as if at what he saw.

Rosalind suddenly turned to look behind.

Michael raised the hammer. His face was wild. His nerves were shrieking. The horror was here. He was in its embrace.

Rosalind turned back again as Michael began to bring the hammer down on her head. In the one second before the oblong of iron crashed against her temple, she had time only to start her arm on a protective journey. The movement looked as though she were drawing a cloak about herself.

The hammer struck.

Her face clicking to blankness, Rosalind sagged and went weaving backwards. She fell into the alcove, landed on her back. Slowly, her limbs straightened to neatness.

For a full minute Michael was lost to his surroundings. He was caught within a swirl of horror and nausea. He was not aware that he had dropped the hammer, had clutched gloved hands to his face, had bent over from the waist and was swaying in time with gasped moans.

Breathing heavily, saliva trickling from his mouth, he stood erect. He retrieved and pocketed the hammer. Face averted, he knelt beside Rosalind and felt under her left breast. There was no murmur.

Michael had done it. He had killed. Success was partly due to the fact that one section of his mind had been insisting, *This is only a rehearsal.*

That he had killed Rosalind instead of waiting to kill Harold was of no consequence. The problem was the act itself. It didn't matter who died. Either one would suffice for his purpose, the aloof and mocking husband, or the wife who had always been kind.

———————————◆———————————

The police car stopped. They had arrived by the portico of Gorse Manor. The journey was over.

Inspector Jack Cartland turned off engine and lights. With a suppressed groan of effort, he eased his bulk out of the car and went toward the house. He reached in his pocket for the key.

Michael Shield alighted. He circled to the far door, opened it, and held it wide. When Mrs. Foster had got out, he offered her his arm, which she took with a smile of thanks and pleasure.

Harold Lunn went to the rear of the car. He lifted the luggage compartment lid and took out the flat box which contained the Ouija board.

Harold was feeling confident. He knew now for certain the police had no case against him; not a case of any power; merely a slovenly collection of circumstantial evidence. On the other hand, he also knew that he was still the number one suspect. That situation, however, could be cancelled with a positive reaction at the seance, either by the board confirming his innocence, or by stating another's guilt: the tramp possibly, John McKay probably.

It was up to Rosalind, Harold thought. If her mind did exist, if discarnate agency were possible, she would come through from the other side. She would come to help.

Taking a tight grip on the slab of box, Harold went over to the steps and up. The others had gone inside. He followed and closed the door. The hall was bright with moonlight, the black and white tiles standing out sharply.

Michael released Mrs. Foster's arm. He went on ahead across the hall. He was remembering, with pride, how he had managed the last time here.

Rosalind dead, Michael had been alone in the house, alone with his terror and the knowledge of that figure downstairs. He had walked slowly. It had been a nerve-shredding three-minute journey from the study to the front door. But he had made it.

Michael smiled. Recovery outside had been swift. His presence of mind had soon returned to him so that, back at the bicycle, he was able to make sure he was plainly seen by a passing car; next, to put the dirt of the roadside in the tread of his tyres; last, to stop at a call box, contact the police, and report a body in Gorse Manor. He had done very well.

Michael began to climb the stairs, still leading the group. Turning right at the fork in the staircase, he glanced back to see if Cartland had noticed that he knew the way.

Inspector Jack Cartland had his eyes on the steps, negotiating them with care. This was automatic. His mind was on the oddness of the situation.

When a seance had been proposed by Harold Lunn, his first instinct had been to decline. But then he had thought, Why not? There was nothing else, there were no avenues left to check, the investigation was at a standstill, and everything pointed to it staying that way.

This, he thought, could well be his last hope. Not that he

believed necessarily in getting a message from the spirit world. He did, however, feel that Harold Lunn might give himself away, or might somehow be shocked into breakdown.

Especially with a little assistance from the pushing finger of Inspector Cartland, the inspector thought.

Jack Cartland's expectations were high. His feeling was strong that tonight, one way or another, he would break the case. And win for himself the grand finale which had come to be his fondest dream.

He plodded on firmly up the stairs.

Michael, walking along the open gallery, was unconcerned that his minor ploy had failed. There had been so many failures during the past week. Nothing had turned out the way he had hoped.

He had thought it was beginning when Inspector Cartland came to the house to ask questions—and his statement about Mr. Lunn's fingerprints being in Gorse Manor had been cleverly weakened with a lie, by telling of Rosalind saying her husband had gone there before. But why hadn't he thought of fingerprints when he was there himself? The terror, that's why.

Michael's next idea was Rosalind's diary. Looking at it, he found that she had not mentioned him by name. He thought this over carefully, and decided that he himself would not be the lover she referred to, but a cuckolded lover. Copying her handwriting, he noted, "Michael will kill me if he finds out." It was perfect. All he had to do was think of a way of getting the book into the hands of the police. But then he had entered the living room to find Mr. Lunn burning the diary. It was all very strange.

An hour after that, hope had risen again when Cartland and other detectives had come with a search warrant. It had been a blow when the inspector, search over, had said, "We're off now, Mr. Shield. And by the way, we didn't look in your room. Under the law, it's your property, not Mr. Lunn's, and isn't covered by the warrant."

"You can search it if you like," Michael had said, thinking of the Gorse Manor key, the hammer, and the gloves, wrapped together and lying under the mattress.

Inspector Cartland had smiled and said, "That won't be necessary."

The following day, Michael had telephoned Mr. Lunn from the hotel about seeing a man buy a hammer. He was surprised the stall-holder hadn't come forward by now. After all, Michael had made quite a fuss when buying the tool a week before, criticising it, haggling over the price. The dealer must have a bad memory. Nothing came of the telephone call.

The next one was better. To Inspector Cartland. Pretending to be a female clairvoyant who'd had a vision of a man digging near the gatehouse. But it turned out badly. Instead of an interrogation at headquarters, he had been treated like a naughty child. And his clever idea of letting the home-made key fall out of his pocket, that had also come to nothing.

However, there was still hope in that direction: the key.

Michael paused by the study doorway to feel in his pocket. He frowned and delved into other pockets quickly. He began to panic.

"Lost something, Mr. Shield?"

He swung around.

Mrs. Foster was approaching. Michael, standing aside, mumbled, "No. Nothing. It's all right."

Mrs. Foster went past and into the study. It was as bright as dawn with the moonlight. Stopping in the middle of the room, the medium gazed around.

She had an intensification of the feeling that had come over her when she had entered the house. It was an indescribable sensation. She didn't know whether it frightened or

caused contentment. It was in every part of her body as well
as in her head.

She thought it could relate to an occult presence in the
house. Or it could simply be the crescendo of the excitement
she had been experiencing ever since this seance was
suggested. She had found difficulty in sleeping. Time and
again she had been taken by the thrilling thought, It will be
the most important night of my life.

Mrs. Foster was highly optimistic. Everything was
favourable for success. She was convinced that here in this
room her dream would come true.

Beside her appeared Inspector Cartland and Mr. Lunn.
The latter asked, "Shall I set the board up, Mrs. Foster?"

"If you would, please."

Harold Lunn went to a table. Its size was ideal—a yard
square. Leaving the box aside, he put the circular board on
the table and positioned it centrally. Two upright chairs already being in position, he brought two others from their
stand by the wall.

Michael finished the third furtive search of his pockets. It
was gone, the key he had made for Gorse Manor. He had
settled it earlier in his handkerchief for a repeat of the per-
formance in the police station. Unthinkingly he must have
pulled the handkerchief out sometime in the afternoon—in
the hotel, walking in town, in a shop.

Michael sighed. He accepted that the key was irretrievably
lost. And it was his last piece of positive evidence.

He sighed, but he was not defeated. There was still hope of
winning. There was the Ouija board. A definite indication
from it of identity, and the police would have to ask more
questions. He would confess. All would fall into place: where
he had bought the file, the market ironmonger, the dirt in his
tyres, the railing fingerprints if they hadn't been washed
away by rain.

Michael moved forward to join the others, who were standing by the table. He avoided looking at the fireplace.

Jack Cartland stopped looking at the mantel of the fireplace and gave his attention to the board. He asked, his voice low:

"What do we do exactly?"

While Mrs. Foster explained, Harold Lunn gazed around the room. His confidence was growing. He thought that possibly never before in the history of parapsychological research had everything been so right, the people so serious, the physically dead so close in time and place.

Mrs. Foster had brought a black Bakelite cup from her pocket. "This is like a small glass," she said. "And that's what we call it, the glass." She also was speaking in a low voice. "We turn it upside down and put our fingers on the top."

The inspector nodded. "I see."

Harold Lunn said, "There has to be body contact between sitters. We touch fingers on the cup or put the left hand on the shoulder of the next sitter."

"It might be best," Mrs. Foster said, "if we did both."

Harold nodded. "I agree."

The medium glanced at each of the three men and asked, "Shall we start?"

Slowly and quietly, the four people sat at the table. Opposite Michael was the inspector, with Mrs. Foster on his left and Lunn on his right.

Beyond Inspector Cartland, Michael could see the chimney piece, and the alcove. It was having company and the fact of his determination which kept his fear to the minimum; the fear which had made him take Mrs. Foster's arm outside, the determination which seconds later had made him go on alone.

The medium said, "Left hands, please."

Each person put his left hand on the shoulder of the next sitter. Michael was further eased by the contact. Inspector Cartland hoped his shoulder-clasp of Harold Lunn was symbolic, a forecast.

The indirect light of the moon shone a silvery glow on the

board. Into its centre Mrs. Foster placed the inverted black cup. She was still experiencing that sensation which might be excitement and which she hoped was not.

A tremble in her voice gave her feelings away as she said, "And now the glass, please."

She and the others reached out to place forefingers on top of the cup. The fingers touched.

After a pause, Mrs. Foster intoned, "Let us keep our minds open and free. Let us not doubt. Let us be welcoming. Let us help those who wish to make this strenuous journey."

She glanced again at the faces of the men. They were grave, committed. Their eyes were on the cross of fingers topping the cup.

Mrs. Foster leaned forward slightly. In a different, soothing yet respectful tone of voice, she asked:

"Spirit of the Glass, will you speak?"

The room abruptly seemed more silent.

Jack Cartland felt the beat of his heart pick up. He had the odd sensation that someone was standing right at his back.

Mrs. Foster gave a light gasp.

It had started, that familiar, slightly aching throb in her arm, accompanied by the dreaminess in her head like post-sleep muzziness. It was an excellent sign.

Slowly, as if reluctantly, the cup began to move. It described a small circle, its rim making a hissing sound on the board's smooth surface.

Fascinated and afraid, Michael watched. He saw the circle widen. The cup hissed around the board at the speed of a slow-turning wheel.

"Spirit of the Glass," the medium repeated, "will you speak?"

The cup broke out of the ring. It went across to *Yes*.

It went there briefly before returning to circling.

Mrs. Foster said, her voice now reduced to a whisper, "Spirit of the Glass, will you please help us make contact with someone who has gone across?"

Again the cup broke away, went briefly to *Yes*, and then returned to circling.

"We wish to contact Mrs. Rosalind Lunn."

The cup began to move at speed, skimming close to the ring of letters. It was like a child who runs around in anger or frustration or the inability to contain joy.

The four sitters had difficulty maintaining their touch on the cup. With the other hand, each person tightened his grip on the shoulder he was holding.

"Rosalind Lunn," Mrs. Foster gasped. "Please help us to find Rosalind."

The cup reduced speed. It moved with a laziness which had an air of assurance, almost of smugness.

Harold Lunn stared at the cross of fingers. His confidence was running strong. Sweat dotted his brow in drops as large as pearls.

The feeling of Jack Cartland's that someone was behind him had grown so fierce he was tempted to look around. What stopped him was fascination in the proceedings.

Michael gripped tightly the shoulder of Mrs. Foster's coat. His other arm was aching with tension. He felt sure that now, the next second, the end would come.

Mrs. Foster, her voice taut, said, "Please, Spirit of the Glass, ask Rosalind who it was who sent her out of this mortal life."

The cup went on circling, but with a ponderousness, as if it were gathering itself for an assault.

None of the three men was aware now of his effort to cheat.

Jack Cartland didn't know he was pushing with his forefinger to send the cup in the direction of L, to begin on the spelling of *Lunn*.

Harold didn't know he was pushing toward M for the spelling of *McKay*.

Michael was not conscious of pressing toward S to start the spelling of his own name, *Shield*.

The cup began to zag and lurch in the centre of the board, making small and aimless patterns. The four fingertips were white around their nails.

"The name," Mrs. Foster whispered. "Please give us the name."

The cup moved away from the middle. It went to the letter L.

Harold Lunn and Jack Cartland stared.

The cup went on. It moved to I, and to B, and to . . .

Mrs. Foster read out each letter and put them together when the cup paused. She said:

"Libertines."

The four people frowned. But briefly. The cup was on the move again, pecking at letters. They formed a sentence.

My feet are wet.

"The name, please," Mrs. Foster whispered.

Each sitter in turn was compelled to sway forward, pulled by his outstretched arm, as the cup chose letters from around the ring. It came to a halt after producing:

He is stopping me.

The medium asked, "Who?"

Moving at an uncertain pace, the cup spelled out, *I want my teddy bear.*

Mrs. Foster said, pleadingly, "Spirit of the Glass, you must help us. Please get Rosalind to tell us who hurt her."

Slowly and deliberately, the cup started again to slide its hissing way back and forth across the board. It touched letters in manifest series, with a curving movement after each one to signal the break. Mrs. Foster spoke each word.

"There.

"Is.

"Something.

"Behind.

"You."

Jack Cartland shuddered.

So did Michael. And his breath caught painfully in his chest. It was that phrase. He had used it to Rosalind.

Fear grew in Michael rapidly.

Harold Lunn became agitated. "Stop this nonsense," he said. "We must have a name, a real name." He released his hold on Michael's shoulder, clenched his fist, and thudded it on the table.

"Rosalind!" he said sharply. "Tell me who killed you!"

"You're spoiling it," Mrs. Foster gasped. "Stop."

The cup was circling, circling.

"Rosalind!" Harold shouted.

The cup began to move swiftly to letters. There was one curving line between the series. Mrs. Foster spoke the two words. She said:

"Little Ben."

With a slap of movement, Michael brought his hand from the medium's shoulder and clamped it to his mouth. The concern for his ambition had gone. Fear was in control. No one but himself knew of that name, knew about his alter ego. Michael shivered in his terror of the supernatural.

Mrs. Foster asked, "Who is Little Ben?"

The cup pecked out, *Nobody*.

Inspector Cartland spoke. He asked, "Who killed you?" *Nobody*.

"A name. Give me a name."

My teddy bear.

Michael took his finger off the cup. He brought the hand to press with the other over his mouth to help in containment.

"Please," Mrs. Foster said. There were tears in her eyes.

The cup glided back and forth across the board. Mrs. Foster and the inspector both read out the words.

"Look.

"In.

"The.

"Corner."

Everyone glanced toward the recess behind the fireplace. It was an empty space—except for Michael Shield.

He saw there a movement. It was a flash, a change of the light, a shifting of dark shadows.

His terror broke through to the surface.

He jumped up and back from the table. His chair crashed aside. He went stumbling backwards. He shrieked:

"Don't let her get me!"

The cup was still.

One by one, the other sitters let their hands fall from it tiredly. Almost as if without interest, they watched the retreat of the young man. All three were listless.

Michael backed away to the wall, slid down it to a sitting position, and drew his knees up to his chest. He began to sob.

Jack Cartland watched drearily. His hope was gone, just as had gone that sensation of having someone stand behind him. He knew now that the investigation was over, the case dead. The killer could have been that tramp, who might have been known as Little Ben. The killer could have been Harold Lunn. The killer could have been the mantelshelf. He would never know.

Jack Cartland sighed bitterly.

Mrs. Foster stared at the sobbing young man across the room. She tried, and failed, to raise compassion for his childish fears. This was to have been the supreme moment of her life, and it had come to nothing. Never again would there be such an opportunity, with place and influences so perfect. That feeling she had experienced: It had, after all, been excitement. The seance had failed. She had failed. The board had produced gibberish.

Mrs. Foster dabbed at her brimming eyes. She was unhappily awake from her dream of absolute knowledge.

Harold Lunn, slumping in his chair, closed his eyes wearily. He accepted that the seance was the last of his chances to prove himself innocent. Although he knew that no one would ever be able to prove he was guilty, that was not enough. He should have been cleared without question. Now the slander would go on living. It would perhaps be less virulent than at present, but always there. He would always bear the brand.

Jack Cartland was the first of the three to rouse himself. Tiredly, he rose and went across the room. The young man had both hands over his face. He was mumbling between sobs.

Poor kid, the inspector thought. He needs looking after.

He knelt before Michael and put a strong grip on his forearms. "Steady on, lad," he said. "You're safe."

"Don't let her get me," Michael whimpered. But already he was losing his terror because of the grip, the human contact.

"You'll be all right, Mr. Shield. I'll see to it that you're taken care of. In a nice safe place where they understand folk like you."

Michael uncovered his face quickly. "What?"

The inspector nodded. "You know the kind of place I mean, son. I'll see to it. You'll be fine. They'll be good to you."

Michael stared.

Jack Cartland said, "They'll be *kind* to you."

Michael began to scream.